I'M NOT YOUR ENEMY

Book 2 of 2

CARA DEE

I'm Not Your Enemy
Book 2 of 2

Edited by Silently Correcting Your Grammar, LLC.
Formatted by Eliza Rae Services.

WELCOME TO THE CAMASSIA COVE UNIVERSE

I'm Not Your Enemy is the second book about Sebastian and Blake, following the first book, *A New Enemy*.

Camassia Cove is a town in northern Washington created to be the home of some exciting love stories. Each novel taking place here is a standalone—with the exception of sequels and series within the CC universe—and they vary in genre and pairing. What they all have in common is the town in which they live. Some are friends and family. Others are complete strangers. Some have vastly different backgrounds. Some grew up together. It's a small world, and many characters will cross over and pay a visit or two in several books—Cara's way of giving readers a glimpse into the future of their favorite characters. Oh, who is she kidding; they are characters she's unable of saying good-bye to. But, again, each novel stands on its own, and spoilers will be avoided as much as possible.

If you're interested in keeping up with secondary characters, the town, the timeline, and future novels, check out Camassia Cove's own website at www.camassiacove.com. There you will also see which characters have gotten their own books already, where they appear, which books are in the works, character profiles, and you'll be treated to a taste of the town.

Get social with Cara
www.caradeewrites.com
www.camassiacove.com
Facebook: @caradeewrites
Twitter: @caradeewrites
Instagram: @caradeewrites

CHAPTER
1

I stuck my feet into my boots as my mother rang the bell and hollered that it was breakfast.

Some things never changed. To this day, breakfast was for everyone who worked on the ranch. A dozen people dropped what they were doing and headed for the main house every morning at seven. Some had just woken up, like me, and others had been up for hours already.

I left my cabin and trailed up the hill like so many times before.

But some things would never be the same either.

Nerves tightened my stomach on the way. Rosie, my old Lab, greeted me on the big porch.

"Hey, girl." I dipped down and kissed the top of her head. "I'll bring you a treat later."

She loved this time of year. The fans weren't necessary anymore, and she could wander around the porch and be lazy wherever she wanted, rather than chasing a shaded spot or a breeze.

Once inside the house, I hung up my hat and entered the big kitchen.

"Mornin', son." Dad briefly looked up from his newspaper.

The others, ten employees and a cousin who was visiting, were busy filling their plates.

Mom didn't spare me a glance. She could pretend it was because she was busy pouring coffee, but we knew better.

It was a punch in the gut and filled me with regret.

I shouldn't have come out to them.

The black sheep of the family had turned an even darker shade of black.

Dad was at the head of the table as always, and no other seat was reserved, but one chair close to Dad was generally saved for me. Today was no exception, so I sat down and reached for a few strips of bacon and two slices of toast.

Ma filled my mug with coffee but didn't ask what was on today's schedule like she usually did. Her regular smile was firmly in place, though. She loved taking care of the people on the ranch, and she flitted about throughout the meal. Her own breakfast would be enjoyed in solitude when everyone was back to work and she had cleared the table. Then she'd sit here with her coffee, toast, and radio. Sometimes, it was Willie Nelson. Sometimes a Christian show.

"Mark, you need to eat more than that," she scolded playfully. "You just sat down!"

"Sorry, ma'am, but we gotta head out," Mark replied. He crammed a muffin into his mouth and gestured to Keith and Ez. They were driving out to the western paddock today, if I wasn't mistaken.

"Thank you for breakfast, Mrs. Kidd," Ez said.

Keith filled in. "Amazing as always, ma'am."

Dad glanced at them over the edge of the paper, then slid his gaze to me. "Were you goin' with them tomorrow?"

I nodded with a dip of my chin. "Yes, sir. I'm fixin' the gate today." The big wrought-iron gate that welcomed people to the Kidd Ranch had taken a hit after a storm last weekend.

"Ah, right." Dad nodded too and returned to his paper. "Good."

The rest of the meal went by with nothing but low murmurs between the ranch hands. I wasn't very hungry, but it was gonna be a long day, and I had to eat.

I sipped my coffee and snuck glances toward Mom every now and then. She was dead set on acting like nothing had happened, wasn't she? She'd burst out in tears and stormed out of the sitting room right after I'd told them two days ago. Since then, I'd been on the receiving end of smiles that didn't reach her eyes and nothing else. She hadn't spoken directly to me at dinner—or breakfast, for that matter.

It was worse than anger. I could take anger.

A few days later, I was working on the fence behind the bed-and-breakfast on our property. The storm had really done a number on us in the most annoying way. Nothing major had been damaged, just a million little things. And when the ranch spanned over four hundred acres, it was a lot of fences that needed to be checked out.

I didn't complain too much. It took me away from the main house area, and that was all that mattered at the moment. I had to bide my time and lie low until my next gig started. Roadwork outside of Atlanta would keep me busy for six months starting on November 1. I was supposed to have another job right now, but it'd been delayed.

At the sound of a truck approaching, I straightened and looked toward the bed-and-breakfast. Dad parked right outside the building and spotted me.

I removed my gloves and reached for my water as he came closer.

Behind the bed-and-breakfast was all green grass and trees. The river had been fenced off about a mile away after too many close encounters from nosy gators. Our guests were here for a ranch experience and for the peace and quiet, not to fall off a horse when it got spooked by a gator.

Personally, I was on any side that drove tourists outta here.

"Lookin' good." Dad nodded at the fence.

I eyed the fence and thanked him.

Was he gonna say something about the other day? He hadn't said anything that day either. On the other hand, he hadn't stormed out or cried. It wasn't in his nature to react outwardly to much of anything. He had a smile reserved for every grandchild, a gruff laugh for every inappropriate joke, and as long as Ma wasn't in the room, he didn't hesitate to cuss at the TV. But that was it.

Dad came to a stop in front of the fence and stuck his hands down into the pockets of his jeans.

"When my daddy told me not to go to war, guess what I did," he said.

I furrowed my brow. "You enlisted."

He nodded once. "When he told me not to buy my own ranch..."

Same story.

I didn't remember my grandfather. I'd just heard stories of him being a mean old dick. Paraphrasing from Mom's recollections. Dad wasn't one to bitch.

"As you know, my family didn't stay together," Dad stated. He was uncomfortable talking about this. He didn't normally get personal. "My sisters are in Texas, Danny's in Milwaukee, Gob in Denver..."

Where was he going with this?

To make it easier for him, I went back to work. It worked for me anyway. When all eyes were on me, my walls went up.

4

"When I met your mother, that was all I wanted," he went on. "A big family that stayed together."

That worked out well, didn't it? The perpetual screw-up, aka me, was the only one who'd stuck around.

"That's why I stole a foolish idea from my daddy," Dad revealed. "Back in the day when I helped out at his law firm, I didn't get paid a nickel. Yet I always had money. I came home to a warm bed, Mama put food on the table, I had new clothes, a nice car... I wanted to keep y'all close, you see?"

Yeah, I was familiar with the concept. I drove a brand-new RAM 1500, I lived for free in one of the guest cabins, and I could put every expense on a black card.

It made me feel like a goddamn child, despite that I would be forty next spring. I'd worked full time my whole adult life, and I had nothing to show for it. Most of it was my fault—I couldn't blame my folks for my career mishaps and shitty behavior—but it still stung not to earn a paycheck from this place. I'd helped my father build it.

"When your brother was eighteen, I started noticin' some strange expenses of his," Dad admitted with a twitch of his mustache. "He was writing checks that made no sense. Why on God's green earth was he buyin' a lawn mower? What did he need tires for? They didn't even fit his truck."

Oh shit. Oh *fuck*. I suddenly had an idea of what this conversation was about.

Blake screws up again.

I kept my stare fixed on the fence and drew a wire to reconnect the net with the post.

"Turns out," Dad chuckled gruffly, "he was paying for crap his friends needed. In turn, they gave him cash."

I was very familiar with that concept, too. It was David who'd given me the idea. My uptight, do-everything-right big brother. Even he had limits, and he'd never wanted to live here longer than necessary. So whenever a buddy was buying something that cost a bit more, David would offer to cover the charge with a check, and they would pay him in cash, slightly under the asking price. Everybody won—except Dad, who was footing the bill. But we'd thought he was oblivious. It was a huge ranch, a big business. Between cattle and horse breeding and the bed-and-breakfast and some other shit, it was impossible for Dad to keep track of it all. He had an accountant in Atlanta, for chrissakes.

"So when you asked him how he'd been able to secure a deposit for his first apartment in Nashville, you already knew," I said.

"'Course I knew," Dad huffed. "I just didn't see the point in sayin' it. I already knew my plan had failed. None'a y'all were destined for a life here, least of all Soph."

I didn't wanna think about her. It only reminded me of another string of failures. I'd let her down. I'd let Teddy down. And it made me think about Sebastian. I'd let him down too.

"I reckon you can cut to the chase, sir," I said and straightened again. "You've caught me doing the same thing David did."

"Several times over the years." He inclined his head. "It's so much easier today too. Did you know I get a text message on my phone every time you charge somethin' over two hundred dollars on the card?"

That was mildly disturbing.

Fuck.

I removed my hat and ran a hand through my hair, and not for the first time in my life, I wanted to be as far away from here as possible. Why the fuck did I keep coming back? Oh, because it was easy, and because I'd gotten fired a lot in the past. It was only in recent years, maybe three or four, that I'd gotten my act together—at least, when it came to work.

"I thought for sure you were leavin' for good this summer

when you went to see Sophia in Washington," Dad told me. "I was real nervous, I admit it. I estimated you'd set aside about a hundred grand at that point."

Hundred and fifty.

I shook my head grimly, admittedly insulted. I supposed I had myself to blame for all the years of lowering their expectations, but I hadn't saved that money for myself. Or spent it, rather, because that money was gone. I'd bought a piece of land in Camassia Cove for Sophia and Dylan to build their dream home. She just didn't know it yet.

"I've no intentions on leavin', sir." While I needed breaks from the ranch and took on short-term leases for apartments around the state wherever work was, I always came back. Sometimes I didn't know why. I wasn't particularly happy here. At the same time, I felt I had a responsibility. David and Soph had left, and Dad needed a right-hand man.

"Well..." Dad rocked a little on his feet, eyeing the fence. "Maybe it wouldn't be a bad idea?"

My brows knitted together. "To what? Leave?"

"Yeah. I...I can't change your mama's beliefs, son."

Beliefs on wh—oh.

So he meant—he actually wanted me to get—

"It's my god's honest truth that I don't care what you do behind closed doors," he went on. "To be honest, I prepared myself already. I used to suspect David was...you know. Never in a million years did I think it would be you, but—here we are."

I couldn't grasp any of the emotions suddenly wreaking havoc within me; I only felt the blood drain from my face, my hearing suffered—it sounded like rushing water—and I couldn't swallow.

He wanted me to leave.

"But you don't have to sneak around with the credit card, is what I'm gettin' at," he added firmly. "I've crunched the numbers, and three hundred thousand dollars should be enough to get you up and runnin' elsewhere. Consider it a token of my gratitude for everything you've done for the Kidd Ranch over the years."

My stomach started churning, pushing nausea up my throat.

"It's just easier this way, Blake."

Easier. Right.

The man couldn't even look me in the eye anymore.

"Mama's been through too much." Now he was making awful excuses. "She doesn't get to see David's kids that often, and now with Teddy not comin' to stay either..."

"Right," I heard myself mutter. Holy shit, they wanted me gone. Because I was the *moron* who'd come out as gay. In this day and age. I mean, I'd known I was going to hurt my mother, but I'd had some hope... That motherfucker—Sebastian. *He* had given me hope. He'd reminded me of the importance of being true to myself. Because if I wasn't honest about who I was, nobody else got the real me either. And all the way home, after running away like a coward, I'd built up confidence that didn't belong there. I'd thought, of course my own mother would want me to be honest. She would love me, regardless.

I'd also known that Dad wouldn't be a big issue. As long as he didn't have to talk about it, he looked past most things.

"I know I haven't always been fair to you, son," he told me. "I've pushed you harder than David and Soph because I see myself in you like I don't do with the other two." He paused. "That's how I know you'll be fine. You're a good man. A hard worker. You stand tall—you're strong. You do what's best for your family."

Was he trying to convince me or himself? Because I was about to fucking blow, and the last thing I felt right now was strong. He'd also never uttered anything like this to me before, partly because I hadn't given him reason to. But now he wanted to push me out the door with a clear conscience.

You do what's best for your family.

He saw himself in me? In other words, he believed he did what was best for his family too?

You do what's best for your family.

As in, leave.

"I will transfer the money and tell your mother you've accepted a job out of state," Dad finished. "She will feel guilty if she thinks you've leavin' because of her."

"But I am," I blurted out. With those words, my pulse went through the roof and hurt slashed through me. "You're kickin' me out because my Bible-thumpin' mother can't handle me being gay."

Dad flinched, only to come back with a narrow-eyed look. "Don't be dramatic. You're not a child, Blake. You're almost forty years old. Surely you can handle livin' on your own."

Like that was the *fucking* issue.

"And we're not kicking you out," he added vehemently. "You're still part of this family. I expect you home every holiday, just like I do with the others, but it'll be—"

"Easier. Yeah. I got that." I was done. I had maybe ten minutes before all the feelings reached the surface, and I wanted to be out of here by then. "Fuck this—give me ten minutes and I'll be gone."

He didn't object.

CHAPTER
2

I made it to my brother's place in Tennessee the next day.
David's wife was out of town with four of their eight
kids, leaving behind the terrifying toddler twins and the two
eldest, who were thankfully calmer. Plus, they liked me the
most.

My brother and I sat on the porch steps and drank beer as
the sun dipped lower and lower over the green hills.

Rosie sat at his feet, enjoying the attention he was giving
her. My prim and proper brother wore a fitted white pullover
from some high-end brand, and the fact that Rosie was an
animal saved her from complaints about shedding. His sleeve
had plenty of little black hairs stuck to the fabric already, but
animals were sacred to him. As they should be, I reckoned,
considering he was a veterinarian.

Meanwhile, I had Oppy and Percy, my Yorkshire terrier
mutts, jumping around on the front lawn. They weren't the
most active pets, but after a day in the car—after a night in a
shitty motel—they reveled in their freedom.

"Dad!" Lee-lee hollered from inside the house. "Can I go
out with Mandy after I give the twins their bath?"

David glanced over his shoulder and spotted his daughter

through the open kitchen window. "You'll be home by ten, deal?"

"Did you say eleven?" she asked hopefully.

I chuckled.

"Fine, but don't tell your mama," David responded, amused.

Lee-lee whooped in triumph, and I was surprised my brother agreed. It wasn't like him.

"Where did that come from?" I asked.

David smiled and took a swig of his beer. "I'm trying to relax."

I raised my brows.

He laughed quietly and scratched Rosie behind her ears. "After eighteen years of being called impossible, difficult, uptight, and rigid by my children—and Mel—I suppose I reached my limit."

Good for him. Hell, good for his entire family.

"Dang. I guess Soph and I were wrong. You *do* listen." It just took him eighteen years.

David grinned.

The humor faded eventually, and he continued. "So are our parents. Wrong, I mean. I can't believe they did this to you." He shook his head. "And if they think we will bring our children to celebrate Christmas with them in a few months, they're sorely mistaken."

I appreciated his support; in fact, I'd always had it on this topic. Sophia's too. But I didn't want them to punish the kids for it. Our folks were still amazing grandparents, which I reminded David of.

"I know," he replied. "But it's way too soon. There have to be some consequences. That's not my Christianity. We say our prayers in this house too, and I don't want my kids to think God doesn't love all his children."

I'd rather steer clear of that entire subject. My relationship with God was complicated enough as it was.

"Have you told Soph yet?" he asked.

I shook my head and finished my beer. "I haven't talked to her in weeks."

I was too embarrassed.

David seemed to know why. "Could it be because you left Washington without a word?"

Dammit.

"It could," I admitted begrudgingly. "I fucked up as usual. Shit got too real, and I split."

"What exactly got too real?" he asked, confused.

I didn't know where to begin, because that was mostly about Sebastian. I still saw him in my dreams every fucking night, but at least I was able to think his name without feeling like anxiety-riddled garbage now. That was something.

"I met someone there," I confessed, and I reached for another beer from the six-pack. "I don't know what the fuck he did to me, but I had to get away. He made me feel shit. Like, physically—" I gestured to my chest. "I swear to God, he gave me chest pains. And my stomach felt like it did in high school before a game. At the same time, I couldn't stop going over to his place. I was obsessed—or possessed. Both fit." I shook my head. "I didn't know what people meant when they bitched about toxic relationships until that guy."

David squinted at me and looked as if he was trying not to laugh. "You think that's the definition of a toxic relationship?"

"Well, yeah. It's when you go back to someone who hurts you."

"Oh my Lord, Blake." He grinned at me, the fucker. "This is the very reason Melissa and I want our children's teachers to go beyond sexual health in school. Anyone can roll a condom onto a banana, but very few understand love."

"What the fuck?" My shoulders tensed up, and I pressed my lips into a thin line. "You're outta your mind if you think I'm in love with that asshole. He *hurt* me. I don't think you understand—fucking *chest pains*, David."

He found that hilarious.

"It ain't funny!" I snapped, getting heated. He was making light of it—I was dead serious. "No man my age deserves to feel that way. Anxiety is for kids who don't know what they're doing."

My brother groaned through a laugh and scrubbed his hands over his face. "I beg to differ, little brother. Especially if you've never felt that way before. It's probably why you reacted so strongly too. The harder they fall..." he mused. "And I didn't say you were in love, you buffoon. But I'm willing to bet you don't know what it's like to develop deeper feelings for someone."

Urgh. I made a face, ready to call off the whole visit and get back on the road.

"If that's what it feels like to develop deeper feelings, I'm gonna have to pass," I said flatly. "Love's supposed to be good. Not...whatever that was." I could barely describe it. Easiest way was probably to compare myself to a teenager. That was how Sebastian had made me feel. Insecure, anxious, un-fucking-glued.

That couldn't be healthy.

David was done laughing, but the humor remained in his eyes. We looked a lot alike, only he wore Ralph Lauren and Armani, and I wore...well, I'd bought this flannel shirt at a fair.

"I hope you see that guy again," he said. "I'll leave it at that."

"That's hateful." I picked at the label on my bottle. "I'll do everythin' in my power to avoid seeing him when I get there."

David perked up at that. "So you're heading back to Washington?"

I shrugged. "I managed to deny it to myself for about four hours yesterday. I told myself I was only aiming for Tennessee." This was after I'd driven aimlessly for a while, just stewing in anger and hurt. "But I don't know. I need a project." It was a sobering thought. I needed a project to get past the fact that my mother couldn't look me in the eye anymore.

"The guy is your project?"

I snorted. "Christ—no. Building Soph and Dylan a home will be."

Something softened in David's eyes.

"I bought them a piece of land," I explained. "When I visited, I asked Dylan when he was gonna make an honest woman out of her—which earned me a kick in the shin from Soph—but he's as bad as she is. They have no plans because every penny has to go to Teddy." I was quick to go on because I didn't want David to get the wrong idea. "You know what I mean. Bad is good and all that, but they're more than parents. Or am I the asshole here?"

David smirked and shook his head. "No, you're not. If I didn't know better, I would call you sweet."

I frowned. "Don't do that."

"No, I know better." He wanted to, though. I could see it on his damn face.

"Anyway." I cleared my throat. "They're stuck in a rat's nest of an apartment, both trying to save up for a better car, a better place to live, all while waiting for promotions—and now the shit with Teddy. They cut the aid for his after-school care group and speech therapy."

"Yes, she told me." David furrowed his brow in disapproval. "She also mentioned you pushed for him to go through a program in Atlanta. Then I heard the rest from Mom after Soph had called the whole thing off. It took me an hour to get Mom to stop crying."

What a clusterfuck that had been. "Mom told me about the program. It seemed obvious to me—even though it was clear as day that our folks used money to shuffle family their way." In the end, Teddy came first, right? Right. And since Soph and Dylan hadn't been able to afford the program, I saw no other option. I would've offered to pay for it myself if I hadn't already bought the land for them. I'd been out of money too. "I don't know how they managed on their own—with the program, I mean. Did she tell you?"

David nodded once, then cocked his head at me as if a thought just struck him. "This guy you met there—was it Sebastian?"

Fuck. I already knew David had met him once. I'd been hoping he wouldn't connect the dots.

"Maybe." I took a swig of my beer while my brother grinned and shook his head.

Out of the corner of my eye, I spied Oppy jumping into Melissa's rosebushes. At the same time, Percy took a shit on the lawn a few feet away.

"Well, he's the one who saved the day," David went on. "Sebastian paid for a similar program in Seattle, which Teddy is currently enrolled in."

Go fucking figure. Sebastian was always the hero.

I let out a whistle for the boys and patted my leg, and Percy and Oppy came running. Or tumbling. Even the most manicured lawn could function as an obstacle for a dog that didn't weigh more than three pounds. But they were so fucking cute. I suspected someone had tried to create one of those trendy Yorkiepoo mixes at some point because their fur was just a tiny bit curly in places, and they were darker than most Yorkies. Smaller too. They were, according to David, right on the lower end of what was considered breed standard.

"Did you know that Sebastian's grandmother was a rather

famous artist?" David asked. "Or semifamous, perhaps. But she had a following, nonetheless."

I quirked a brow. "I knew she painted and opened a youth center."

David hummed. "Apparently, Sebastian sold some of her paintings to pay for Teddy's program. Soph was shocked—six paintings went for over twenty grand."

Hot fucking damn.

"All of it went to Teddy," David went on. "Sebastian wouldn't keep any of it, despite that the program cost less than half of what he received."

What the hell was David doing? I got it; Sebastian was great. He was fantastic. He was the best.

Jealousy ignited within me, and I wondered if Washington could be more than a temporary place to forget the rejection of my parents. What if I moved there? It'd been so good to see Teddy every day when I visited. No offense to David's brood— he had great kids, but they were programmed to find grown-ups embarrassing as soon as they hit eleven. Teddy turned twelve on Halloween and still greeted me with the biggest grins and tightest hugs.

I wanted what Sebastian had with my nephew.

"Hmm." David frowned at Rosie. "Mind humoring me with a checkup at the clinic tomorrow?"

What—oh. "You mean the lump on the inside of her leg?" I asked. "We already checked it out. It's just a lipoma." A fancy word for a lump of fat.

"No, this is something else," David murmured. He gathered Rosie between his legs and felt along her ribs, then up to behind her ears. It put me on edge right away. "You're a beautiful girl, aren't you?" He leaned forward and pressed a kiss to Rosie's nose. "Have you noticed any changes in her behavior? How's her appetite?"

Fuck no, I wasn't doing this. "She's fine," I insisted. "She's tired—she's getting older. That's normal." I swallowed hard as a memory struck. Yesterday, before we hit the road, she hadn't jumped up into the truck. I'd had to lift her. But that was normal too. As I'd said, she was getting older.

"Her appetite, Blake."

I sighed and quickly grew frustrated. "I don't know, I guess she eats less these days—but not by a lot, and Mom still gives her food on the sly." Or she had, up until yesterday.

"Well, it could be nothing." David cranked up the reassurance in his tone; only, the damage was already done. Now I wasn't gonna be able to sleep. My stomach tightened with nerves, and anxiousness constricted my chest. "I just want to make sure. Better safe than sorry, right?"

"But something triggered this," I argued. "What's wrong with her?"

"I don't know yet," he responded patiently. "Her lymph nodes are swollen, but there could be a number of reasons."

"I swear to Christ, you're the grim reaper, David. This is Grits and Blitz all over again!"

I got my first dog at nineteen, around the same time David was in veterinary school, and he was the one who suspected Grits was sick. After two expensive weeks at the clinic, my pup was put down because of a birth defect in his lungs.

Twelve years later, it was my second dog's turn. David discovered Blitz's cancer.

"We shouldn't have come here," I said irritably and picked up Oppy. I didn't want him to go near my brother. "You stay with Daddy now, you hear? David gives you cancer and broken lungs."

Oppy merely wagged his tail and breathed excitedly, tongue poking out.

We were at David's clinic first thing next morning, arriving ten minutes before his overzealous assistant Benjamin. Benjamin hit on me every time I visited, but the kid was barking up the wrong tree. We had the same taste in men.

Maybe Sebastian would like him.

Under normal circumstances, David let family members be present during most exams—as long as the owner's energy contributed to a calm atmosphere. Since mine clearly didn't, I was banished to stay behind in the waiting room.

I wasn't equipped to handle shit like this. Relationships, I could run away from. Hell, I'd never really had one. Parents, I could avoid—even more so when they didn't even want me around. Jobs, I could quit. But my dogs? My dogs were my world. The only creatures I surrendered my heart to willingly and unconditionally. My siblings and nieces and nephews were the exception, though that was different. I didn't need them for my everyday well-being. I didn't have to see them every day. Rosie, Percy, and Oppy were my own little family. I depended on them almost as much as they depended on me.

I did need Soph now, though. She had a calming aura about her.

My knee bounced restlessly as I fidgeted with my phone and glanced toward David's exam rooms. He had two of them and one area for surgery.

By now, Benjamin had taken his spot behind the desk and was eating yogurt for breakfast.

I released a nervous breath and scrolled down my messages until I found Soph. Last I'd heard from her were a few angry texts after I'd left Washington.

I didn't wanna call her, considering the hour. It was too early in Camassia. Plus, they had Isabella. She was what, two months old now? Something like that. After David and Melissa's fifth child, I'd stopped keeping track of ages and birthdays.

I opted to text Soph instead.

Except, I didn't know what to type. My thumb hovered over the keyboard as I racked my brain for the right words. Did I start with an apology? I couldn't do that. Judging by the number of times I'd messed up in my day, one might think I was used to handing out apologies, but I wasn't. When I asked for forgiveness, it was a big deal to me, and it sure as heck didn't happen over the phone or in a text.

I'd never apologized for ignoring a curfew or coming home wasted as a kid. I'd never apologized for being late to work—or for not showing up at all and then getting canned. Nor had I apologized for bailing in the past. My family knew that about me, and it wasn't where they counted on me. I drew a line in the sand for each case, and I picked my battles based on what hurt others. And how much I cared. I didn't fucking care about the employer who ignored safety measures in order to get the job done faster. Fuck him. I also hadn't cared about stumbling home at the crack of dawn to find my father waiting on the porch with a glare in place.

That was part of growing up.

When I apologized, it was because I knew I'd crossed a line that genuinely hurt others. An apology from me was also a guarantee that whatever I'd done would never happen again.

To David, that line was drawn at baptisms. It was the one occasion that meant the world to him. So after I'd missed his eldest daughter's baptism and seen how it had affected him, I'd asked for forgiveness and never missed another one.

My mother had never been able to handle shit-talk about her religion. She took that incredibly personally, so I'd apologized the time I, uh, I hung a pentagram on the mantle. She hadn't appreciated that joke one bit.

Soph... I owed her a big apology for lying to her. I knew how much she valued her friendship with Sebastian, and I had promised I was going to tell him about the program for Teddy that Mom had found in Atlanta. And I never did. I'd chickened out because I'd known that Sebastian was gonna flip.

Lying was the one thing you didn't do to my sister. It was why she'd been the first one I'd come out to over ten years ago. She'd overheard me on the phone with some guy.

I guessed talking to her was gonna have to wait until I got to Washington.

I pocketed my phone again and bit at a cuticle.

"I'm sure your dog will be fine, Blake," Benjamin said.

I hated sugarcoating and empty words, so I couldn't bring myself to acknowledge him. If Rosie turned out to be sick, there wasn't a whole lot I could do. She was almost eleven years old. At best, she had another three years. Which was enough to throw money at if it was something that could be cured. But I'd been around dogs my whole life, and... Fuck. I wasn't ready to lose her.

I stayed at my brother's place for a week while we waited for the results to come back, and he'd prepared me for the worst. He'd been honest with his suspicions, and I loathed that he turned out to be right.

I knew that before he even told me, because he came home in the middle of the day when the kids were in school or day care, and he sat down with me on the porch steps.

"It's cancer, innit?"

He nodded once. "She has an aggressive type of lymphoma."

"Fuck." My throat closed up, and I brought Rosie close to

me. I hugged her to me, pressing my face against her neck, and couldn't stop the emotions from spilling over. Fuck this mother-fucking fuck! Rage tore through me, every bit as powerful as the grief that welled up, and I didn't wanna believe it. She was *fine*. She was wonderful. She was the best dang dog a guy could ask for.

I sniffled and inched away to get a look at her, and she was as pretty as the day I adopted her. Shiny black coat. Big beautiful eyes. And so loyal and comforting. And smart—a good worker in the field. She'd been there with me, every step of the way, the past decade. It was only the last year she'd taken up permanent residence on the big porch of the main house. Before then, she'd stayed with me in one of the guest cabins or whatever apartment I was leasing at the time I worked away from the ranch.

"I'm deeply sorry, brother," David murmured. "I can refer you to an oncologist if you'd like to get started on a treatment. The odds are usually pretty good for the cancer to go into remission."

I hated that word. It brought false hope. "And nine times out of ten, the cancer comes back within a year."

"Not quite those numbers, but..." He dipped his chin, conceding, because in the end, lymphoma was terminal.

I stroked Rosie gently behind her ears and felt more tears roll down my cheeks. "Is she in pain?"

"No." He reached out and touched her neck.

Rosie did what she'd done so many times before. She licked David's hand and planted a paw on my knee in comfort.

"There's no one like you, sugar." I leaned down and kissed the side of her face. "What is your honest recommendation for her?"

David sighed and rested his arms on his legs. "In her specific case...? Given her age and how aggressive the cancer is, I probably wouldn't prolong things. And without treatment, she has maybe two or three weeks before she'll be in pain."

Because the cancer would spread and ultimately cause organ failure. Yeah, I was painfully familiar with that part.

"Goddammit." I wiped at my face and tried to get my shit together. "I need family members who don't fucking die every ten years."

David put a hand on my back. "There's an idea."

He didn't have to spell it out. He and Soph had encouraged me to spend more time with people than animals, no matter how much they loved animals too.

I'd thought adopting Oppy and Percy had been a decent compromise, because smaller dogs lived longer than bigger breeds. My brother and sister had humored me.

I released a breath and brushed my fingers over Rosie's paw. "I want you to do it before I leave."

Part of me wanted to bring her along with me to Washington—have a final adventure with me—but I couldn't risk her being in pain.

"Of course." David squeezed my shoulder. "We don't have to do it at the clinic either."

I liked that idea. Rosie had always loved the small barn behind David's house. They'd renovated it and turned it into a playground, complete with a slide from the hayloft, monkey bars, and seating area for children's birthday parties. With eight kids, it was just a solid investment.

I dipped down and pressed my forehead to the top of Rosie's head. "Daddy loves you, Rosie. Always remember that, okay? I love you, I love you, I love you."

CHAPTER
3

I was actually trading the best time of year to be in the South for this...this frigid, wet, evergreen dump.

Perhaps frigid was a stretch, but in October, you could still wear a T-shirt in my part of Georgia.

"I'll have to dress y'all up like them Hollywood dogs, won't I?" I reached over to the passenger's seat, and Oppy tumbled into my touch. It would be just my luck if a cop pulled me over now. Five days of being good, of the boys riding in their carrier in the back, but now because Daddy was depressed and wanted company the last few miles, some officer was gonna jump out of the woods and put me away for life. I could see it happening.

I drove past the sign welcoming me to Camassia Cove and felt that was a bit presumptive. I knew of at least two people who didn't want me here.

I rolled down the window and shivered at the cold, but we might as well get used to it. We were sleeping in the truck until I got the guesthouse up and running. And I had to hurry. I couldn't imagine anyone building houses in northern Washington past October. Thankfully, the guesthouse was one of those pre-cut cabin kits I'd ordered—230 square feet, fourteen grand. Shouldn't take me more than a couple weeks to assemble if I worked full time.

Two weeks was approximately what I had before I'd force myself to let Soph know I was in town, because that was Halloween and, more importantly, Teddy's birthday.

I drove through the town and followed the signs for Downtown. In my experience, downtown was run-down and unsafe or part of a financial district in a major city. Here, it was idyllic Victorian suburbia forming a crest around a small town center and a marina.

The lot I'd found was on the eastern outskirts, essentially as far away as one could get from the marina that jacked up the prices in the area. Past the last houses on Marten Lane, blurring the line between civilization and forest, I found the place.

I was so used to thinking in terms of acres, but that wasn't possible here. 16.000 square feet of overgrown grass, shrubs, and a few trees. The back of the property was cut off by boulders and a cliffside that melted into the forest, creating a natural fence that a kid certainly couldn't climb. Still, I pulled out my pocket-sized notebook from the glove box so I could jot down safety netting. We couldn't risk falling rocks.

"All right, boys. Welcome to our temporary home, I guess." I dropped the notebook on my lap and drove past the property line, making sure I didn't hit anything on the way in. The best part of the deal was that all utilities were ready and waiting at the edge of the lot—water, electricity, gas, sewer. Permits were in place too.

This was gonna be good for me. Something to take my mind off Rosie and my folks.

There were times I definitely didn't mind waking up to the feel of a tongue on my skin. Spending the nights at Sebastian's place came to mind, for instance. He came to mind way too often...

This was nowhere near as exciting, unfortunately. I just had two dogs that needed their morning walk.

"All right, all right." I grunted and sat up, and I squinted at the orange canvas above me. Rain was splashing down on the tent, as it had for the past three days I'd been here.

Pop-up tents for trucks were a brilliant idea if you were going hiking. You could sleep in the bed of your truck and make it real comfortable—but when it wouldn't stop raining, it got old fast. I couldn't work. I couldn't use the grill I'd bought and set up right outside. Unless I bought an umbrella... I'd do that later today.

After pulling on my jeans, I stuck my feet into my boots and opened the canvas door. Raindrops hit my shoulders. It was cold too. Fucking hell, we weren't in Georgia anymore. Then I lifted out the boys and let them do their thing on the lawn. Or what would be a lawn.

I rolled my shoulders and reached for a tee inside the truck, followed by my jacket and Bulldogs ball cap. According to the weather forecast, it was going to be a nice weekend, and I was ready to work at full speed around the clock if I had to.

Everything was here. Equipment, the cabin kit, supplies— I'd gathered it all under tarps along the fence of the only next-door neighbor around.

I took a big breath and inhaled the forest. It was probably what I liked the most about Washington. Not getting bit up by red fire ants and the forest. Rosie and I used to hunt deer together in the fall; she'd been an amazing partner, and she'd loved the woods too.

"Daddy's ready for breakfast," I declared. "We're gonna check out some nearby hiking trails later too. Y'all lazy little shits need to exercise."

Oppy and Percy yipped and ran around my feet as I grabbed my essentials from the tent. With a snap of a string, the top of the tent collapsed, and I was able to roll the cargo cover over the whole thing. Then I picked up the boys and opened the door to the back. My belongings fit into four duffels that filled the floor, and it kind of worked out. With the bags creating an extension to the seat, I'd bought a travel pen that fit perfectly and gave the dogs room to move around. And I didn't have to worry about them falling between any cracks or whatever.

I was a worrier when it came to these two rascals. They were basically rats.

Once I'd strapped their carrier into place, I got behind the wheel and peeled out of there.

Daddy needed a shower today too. I fucking reeked.

"Maybe a hotel wouldn't hurt one night," I muttered to myself. Did they even have hotels in this tiny-ass town?

The goddamn rain made everything worse. It caused me to wake up in a bad mood, and not being able to work made my mind wander. I'd almost driven over to Sebastian's house on the beach last night.

I needed *something* to do.

I drummed my fingers along the wheel and drove through the stretch of forest that led to a neighborhood called Cedar Valley. Soph had once recommended a couple gay-friendly bars there. It reminded me of a miniature version of Seattle, and I could admit they had some fantastic food in the area. They knew their burgers and their seafood.

I slowed down before I reached a stoplight, and if anything, the rain was picking up. I shook my head and peered out the windshield. This was gonna make me crack. Today was the day. If I didn't find anything useful to do, I was gonna seek out Soph or Sebastian. Or I would start stalking his social media.

In my opinion, I deserved a fucking medal for staying away for so long. After all, we followed each other on Instagram— unless he had blocked me, which was highly possible—and we'd friended each other on Facebook back when everything was great.

What was he up to? In the summer, he spent a lot of time working at his grandfather's orchard, but that had to be over for the season, right?

On my way to a coffee shop Dylan and Soph had introduced me to this summer, I passed a sports bar and decided I was gonna treat myself to dinner there next Falcons game. If I wasn't mistaken, we were playing the Seahawks right before Halloween. Maybe we could stop our losing streak... We hadn't won a game since Philly.

Following the Bulldogs was a hell of a lot more rewarding, and I *had* to have a TV installed somewhere by November, 'cause we had three big games next month.

"For being a dead li'l town, they barely have any available parking." Was I asking too much, huh? Was that it? Rain, no parking, no proper bed—fucking hell. All I wanted was my folks' acceptance, my Rosie with me, and a seventy-inch flat-screen, and I couldn't even get a little bit of sunshine. "Fuck it." I swerved into a loading zone and looked around me. "Daddy will be right back." Then I left the truck and jogged toward the coffee shop.

I *hated* the rain.

I needed a roof... A roof. That was fucking it. Of *course*— that's what I had to do. I'd head on over to the store and pick up more tarps after breakfast. If this shitty town wasn't gonna ease up on the rain, I'd build the guesthouse under a roof.

Thank God for small favors, there was no line at the shop. I was in and out in two minutes and hurried back down the cobblestone sidewalk with a large coffee, a bagel with cream cheese, and a treat for the boys.

Back in the truck, I reached between the seats and let them

out of the carrier. "I got y'all a meatball sandwich the way you like it—no bread, no lettuce, no cheese, no sauce."

I pulled out my pocketknife and cut one meatball into tiny pieces and let them go nuts, saving the other two for later. Their little stomachs couldn't handle a whole lot.

Okay, I could do this. A roof, yeah—first break I'd caught since I got here. I nodded to myself and took a sip from my coffee.

A couple knocks on the window interrupted my brief peace, and I jumped in my seat. "Jesus, Mary, and Joseph!" If I was getting a ticket now, I was gonna flip my ever-loving—*fuck*. A glance out the window revealed something much worse.

Dylan.

His forehead creased, and his gaze flashed with equal parts confusion and amusement.

I rolled down the window. "I was hoping to avoid this."

"Then you probably shouldn't get breakfast right across from the place where I work," he responded, not missing a beat. "Am I missing something here? Soph didn't mention you were coming back so soon."

I really wanted to hate this guy. If he'd been a lousy piece of shit, I could've told him to mind his fucking business. Instead, he was everything Soph needed and then some. Hardworking, ambitious, faithful, nice as hell, definitely easy on the eyes... More than that, he'd become a terrific daddy to Teddy.

"She doesn't know I'm here," I admitted. How much did I tell him? Preferably as little as possible, but I had to go one of two routes. Either I told him the gist of what'd led to my hasty move across the country, and I didn't think unloading on my future brother-in-law—whom I'd met all of one time—about my folks was appropriate. Or, I let him in on my plan for the land I'd bought.

"Then *why*, Blake?"

Right, he was protective too. A good trait. And right now, I was the fuckup brother who'd let down his girlfriend and the mother of his two kids.

I raked my teeth over my bottom lip and reckoned I didn't have a choice. "I'll show you. Just—don't tell Soph yet. Meet me at the end of Marten Lane in Downtown when you get off work."

He narrowed his eyes, understandably puzzled and possibly suspicious.

"Don't tell Sebastian either."

That earned me a snort, and Dylan took a couple steps back. "He'd bite my head off for even saying your name."

Ouch. But I'd seen that coming. I wasn't a popular guy around these parts.

Hell, I wasn't popular anywhere.

This was starting to look a lot like a construction site. When I'd failed to attach the tarp to the mountainside, I'd managed to track down a local scaffolding contractor who'd had what I needed. Now, three pieces of tarp created a 300-square-foot roof over the corner of the property where the guesthouse would be.

I'd nearly fallen off the ladder twice, almost broken my arm when I'd slipped in the muddy grass, it'd all cost me three grand, and my clothes were soaked by rain and mud, but whatever.

I was happy about taking the opportunity to rent the spotlights attached to the scaffolding too, 'cause now I didn't have to stop just because it got dark.

"What the hell, Blake?"

I spun around and spotted Dylan coming out of his car. "Hey."

Percy and Oppy barked but stayed in the truck. Like me, they were fucking done with the rain. I had the door closed but the window rolled down a bit, and I wasn't surprised to find the boys cuddled up in blankets outside their carrier.

I met Dylan behind the truck, only to come to an abrupt halt when Soph was next to step out of their car.

Shock turned me rigid, and I couldn't look away from her to save my life. Fuck, fuck, fuck. I wasn't ready. I hadn't worked on my apology yet. God*dammit*. I couldn't help but flick Dylan a quick glare, but I was back to staring at my sister a second later.

Of course he'd told her. Unlike me, he didn't lie to her.

"Howdy, stranger." Soph was feigning a casual expression, only the tightness around her eyes betraying what lay underneath.

I swallowed.

She zipped up her jacket and joined Dylan's side.

"This is unusual behavior even for you," she told me. "Why are you back? Is this a jobsite?"

Kind of?

"I, uh..." I glanced over my shoulder, then back at the two of them. "It's a project," I replied lamely. Too vaguely. She'd never accept it. "Fuck—I wasn't prepared to see you."

She lifted her brows. "That makes two of us."

"Some answers, maybe?" Dylan threw that out there.

And I'd had it. I blew out a frustrated breath and thought, fuck it. *Here goes.* "I had to get outta Georgia for a while, and this was the only place I could think of." I went on, ignoring Soph's evident confusion because I couldn't blame her. Every other time I'd "had to get away," I'd never ended up here. "I need something to do—something to keep my mind off other shit, and I had this gift..." I shook my head quickly, getting it all wrong. The words came out wrong. I had to start over. "About a week after I got here this summer, I bought this piece of land for

32

y'all. I was hoping to make it an early wedding gift." It was almost comical how both their hairlines rose with the lift of their eyebrows. "I was gonna tell you before I left, but..." But I'd run away like some kid. "Now I'm here for selfish reasons," I continued. "On the flip side, I'm hoping you'll find this works out in your favor. Instead of waiting to be approved for a loan so you can build on the property, I'll get started for you. In fact, I'm hoping to stay until it's finished next year."

They were just staring at me. Should I say something else? They put me on edge, goddammit. More than I already was.

"Obviously, I can't build the whole house myself," I said. "I'll bring in contractors as soon as winter's over, but I'll get the guesthouse ready in a couple weeks." I jerked my thumb over my shoulder. "I'm starting on the foundation tomorrow. Lights, heaters, fans, and gravel's being delivered at—"

"*Hold up.*" The words gusted out of Soph. "You're saying this is for us? Blake, we can't afford—"

"It's all taken care of," I replied quickly. I didn't want her to think about the money. "The lot is already yours—I just gotta sign it over into your name. And the rest—don't worry about it. The plans are in place. The house will look like the others on the street. Sixteen-hundred square feet, two stories, four bedrooms, two and a half baths. And, look." I hurried to the passenger's side of the truck and retrieved some samples I'd collected. "I know money's tight, yeah? So we're going all out. The back of the roof will have solar panels, and this—" I extended a booklet of sorts that contained samples of various types of insulation. "The fourth one—it'll lower the costs of heating the place from underneath. It's why I decided on a conditioned crawl space. Unless you object, I mean."

"Jesus." Dylan scrubbed a hand over his mouth and flipped through the samples.

"I don't know what that means, and I can't find the words."

33

Soph became weepy. "How is this happening? Who's paying for all this? Did you win the freakin' lottery?"

Sure. I won the queer lottery and got some hush money.

"Dad gave me the money," I said.

Soph made a sound of disbelief. I realized the questions were gonna keep piling up until I had no choice but to admit everything, but it was a shitty time and place. The annoying drizzle, the darkness falling, and the fact that I was soaked all the way through made me wanna call it a day and check in to a nice hotel with a bathtub.

I still hadn't gotten my shower.

"First of all, Dad doesn't give away money," Soph stated. "Second of all, why would he give you money to build Dylan and me a house?"

Fuck my life. I suppressed a sigh. "Is there any way we can talk about this tomorrow? I haven't showered in four days, I'm so fucking over the rain in this godforsaken state, and my balls just crawled back inside my body because it's so cold."

Dylan glanced around the site before he looked back at me. "Please tell me you're staying at one of the inns in the area."

"I would love to, but I've been roughin' it." I nodded at the bed of the truck. "I got one of those tents for trucks. It's all right."

"Christ—I wish I'd known, man. We can help you out," Dylan said.

"I appreciate it, but my air mattress is actually comfier than your couch." I was too tired to be kind about their ratty couch.

He shook his head. "That's not the only option. Give me one hour—I'll be back." He turned to Soph and murmured something in her ear, then kissed her cheek, and she nodded and smiled. A genuine smile I hadn't seen in quite some time.

When Dylan was halfway back to the car, Soph yelled out

for him to wait, and she rushed after him. To get her purse, apparently.

One hour. I could hold out for that long, right? One hour alone with my sister.

My stomach chose that moment to rumble a reminder about the fact that I hadn't eaten all day.

I supposed it was as good a time as any to fire up the grill. I had a roof now and everything. It would be nice to get warm too.

"Can we sit in the truck?" Soph asked.

"I have a better idea." I had a foldable camping chair in the back of the truck, and I'd bought two plastic lawn chairs. "There's a cooler on the floor of the passenger's seat. Mind grabbing it? I'm starving."

In the meantime, I carried over the chairs, the grill, and then went back to the truck to pop the tent. Because I needed to get out of my wet clothes. It couldn't wait. While I was back there, I snatched the bag of charcoal too, along with lighter fluid, a towel, and a roll of black trash bags.

"I can hear the squishing in your boots, Blake."

"Wanna smell them?"

"Oh my God."

I grinned and dropped the change of dry clothes in the camping chair.

Soph was suddenly in full nesting mode and didn't need to be told what to do. After dumping coal and lighter fluid into the grill, she fanned out three trash bags on the ground to create a makeshift floor. It would get messy in no time, but it beat standing in the actual mud.

This was gonna be freezing. I shed my jacket, hung it over the back of a chair, and then stripped down to just boxer briefs. I put my boots back on too, though.

"You're out of your damn mind," she told me. "This isn't like running through the summer storms in Georgia."

I was surprised she remembered. She'd always gotten scared at the first crack of thunder and hightailed it back to the house.

"Don't have much of a choice." Besides, I didn't mind. I was pretty good at making do. As long as I got clean.

I stepped out from under the roof and into the rain. For once, I was glad it was picking up. Otherwise, it was gonna take forever to wash off. Speaking of, I should grab my soap.

I trailed back to the truck once more, and I figured it was best to give the boys some extra heat too. Soap in one hand, a disposable hand warmer in the other, I opened the door to Oppy and Percy and activated the little pad.

"This is one of those times Daddy wouldn't mind weighin' three pounds," I murmured. They looked all snuggly in the blankets and stretched sleepily as I slipped the heater underneath the top layer. "There we go." I picked up some of the kibble they'd dropped around their bowl.

I closed the door carefully so as not to startle them before I refocused on my very lovely, high-standard shower in the cold rain.

It didn't really compare to a bathtub, if I was honest.

"Will you be offended if I drop my unmentionables?" I asked.

"No, but you will be when I gag."

Nice. Screw her, I was cleaning my junk too. So I walked behind the truck and got to it.

"You're doing it!" she hollered.

"Quit thinkin' about me naked—it's weird!" I called back.

It would be awesome if this was how we met Soph and Dylan's future neighbor, just as I dragged the bar of soap under my balls, something I had no issue saying out loud—emphasis on loud—to Soph.

I was met with silence when I'd expected a familiar shriek or at least some bitching.

"I swear my brain functioned better when I was pregnant," I heard her say instead. "Is this really happening, Blake? Are you building a house for us?"

I shuddered violently at the cold, the rain picking up further. It was fucking pouring down.

"I promise, honey. It'll be done next summer." I tossed the soap near the back tire and rubbed my hands along my torso to get rid of the suds. "I looked into safety netting along the cliff-side earlier today. There're kinds designed to look more like a trellis. That'd be neat, wouldn't it?" Nothing ruined the natural look like a damn fence, so it would be cool to cover it in vines and whatnot. Mom was obsessed with climbing roses; I knew Soph had liked them too.

"It's overwhelming." Soph's voice was nearly drowned out by the rain. "I still don't understand the bit about money. I don't believe it. That's not Dad's way of helping."

I sighed and squeezed as much water out of my underwear as possible, then pulled them up again. If I was gonna tell her everything, maybe now was the best time—when we weren't face-to-face.

"I came out to them," I confessed. "Mom reacted like I knew she would. Dad didn't say much, but a few days later, he offered me three hundred grand to start fresh somewhere else."

Embarrassment burned through me. I couldn't help it. This wasn't like all the times I'd come home drunk or when I'd failed a test. It wasn't the same as stealing Dad's car, getting caught smoking pot, or getting fired. This was *me*. Just by being myself, I was an inconvenience, and it hurt more than I wanted to admit.

"Tell me you're joking," Soph gritted out. "He did not do that."

I swallowed hard and tilted my face skyward, grateful for the darkness, grateful for the rain that washed away everything I didn't wanna show. *You do what's best for your family.* What a farce.

"Blake," she pleaded.

I cleared my throat and wiped at my cheeks before stepping out of the dark. The growing fire in the grill cast glowing shadows on the cliffside behind Soph, and it was easy to see the devastation in her eyes.

"Don't cry, sis." I pushed back my hair and shivered as rivulets of icy water made their way down my back. It was definitely time to get warm and dry.

"I hate them," she croaked. "I'm never talking to them again."

"Shush. We save our hate for Georgia Tech." As soon as I was under the roof, I snatched up the towel and began drying off. "They're still our folks. Teddy and Isabella's grandparents."

She scoffed at that. "See if I fucking care. I'm not having my kids near them if they can't accept you for who you are. I know you're all—" She waved a hand, dismissive. "You know, respect everyone's opinion and whatever—and fine. They'll have to respect my opinion then, too, and they can go to hell. Teddy and Isabella are my children, and I decide what kind of people I want around them."

I wasn't gonna argue with her when she was upset. Right now, I didn't have it in me to defend our folks either.

"Cover your delicate eyes." I stepped out of my boots and boxer briefs, to which she squeaked and spun around to find the cooler highly interesting. Not a whole lot was in there—two packs of hot dogs, hot dog buns, mustard, a couple beers, and the boys' leftover meatballs.

It was an amazing feeling to put on a pair of dry underwear and sweatpants. A hoodie followed quickly, and then I repositioned one of the chairs closer to the grill. As soon as my ass landed in the camping chair, I could aim my feet toward the heat.

"Speaking of my little niece," I said. "Where is she?"

"With Dylan's mom." Soph put the hot dogs on the grill before sitting down next to me. "I'd invite you to come with us to Seattle tomorrow to pick up Teddy, but Sebastian's comin' too..."

I drew in a deep breath, bugged by the return of the Sebastian Stab, as I'd come to call it. After I'd left Washington last time, it felt as if someone took a knife to my chest every time his name flitted through my thoughts.

"It's fine." It didn't feel fine, but it would. Eventually. "I reckon he wants to see me about as much as I wanna see him."

She turned to me at that, and her brows knitted together. "Do you have a reason for not wanting to see him?"

For real? Christ. Well, buckle up, sis. I had a story for her, and unlike David, our sister knew what a toxic relationship was. So I told her what I'd told him. I emphasized for good measure. I mentioned the chest pains I'd had, how he'd unnerved me every goddamn time I saw him, the anxiousness, the uncertainties that'd appeared out of nowhere. And the sickness. The twisted obsession and ever-present urge to go back to what clearly harmed me.

She probably needed to process once I was done, because she kept looking at me like she was waiting for the punch line. I reluctantly moved my feet from the chair across from me so I could stand up and turn the hot dogs, which should be done in a minute or two.

"I'm sorry, I..." She shook her head as if to clear it. "So—I mean... Wow. So that's why you don't want to see him?"

"Ain't that enough?" I asked in disbelief.

She widened her eyes at me, and humor seeped into them. "Uh, *no*, attraction jitters and fear of fallin' in love are reasons

39

to see him *more*, you wackadoo." Her words caused me to recoil, and I couldn't fucking believe her. But she wasn't done. "Under normal circumstances, I would've jumped straight into playing matchmaker, because God knows y'all're perfect for each other—you're both busy acting like morons at the moment—but Teddy comes first. He worships the ground you walk on, and he'll be so happy when he hears you're staying." At that, she cocked a brow. "If that's what you're actually doing."

It sobered me up, and I faced her fully for this. I'd improvise my apology. "I'm stayin', Soph. And I'm very sorry I've given you reason to doubt that. No more chickenin' out from me. I was in over my head, and the last thing I wanted was for that to affect you and Teddy—and Dylan, for that matter." I could imagine him cleaning up my mess and being there for Soph and Teddy. "It won't happen again, honey. No lies either. I'm so sorry."

She smiled a little and squeezed my hand. "I've never received the famous Blake Kidd apology before. I forgive you."

The relief poured into me like a nice river on a hot summer day, and I leaned over and kissed her cheek. "Thank you."

Unless we wanted to eat burned hot dogs, it was time to take them off the grill, so I flipped the lid of the cooler and used it as a platter.

"I'm really happy you're staying, Blake. *Finally*, I'll have someone to go watch games with," she said with a giddy smirk. Hell, I mirrored it. I missed watching football with her. "I know just the spot, too. I didn't get to show you last time, but there's a place in the Valley—the owner's from Savannah."

"Fuckin' A." That was fantastic. "Maybe it's the place I drove by this mornin'."

"It couldn't have been, because there would be no doubt," she chuckled. "The windows are completely filled with bumper stickers for Southern teams—except for Alabama. No Crimson Tide, no Auburn."

"I love the place already." I grinned and shook the mustard.

Conversation lulled as we prepared our hot dogs, and Soph brought out the two bottles of beer too. They were still cold, thank fuck. Christ, how the day had turned around on me. Here I was, thawing out in front of a fire, having hot dogs and beer with the best sister in the world.

"Man, oh man. This beats the chicken I'm defrosting in the sink," she said with her mouth full. "By the way, before I get off track again. About what I was saying—Teddy comes first. You and Sebastian will have to figure out your crap on your own, but I demand a truce when Teddy's around. Y'all're so important to him, Blake. You better play nice."

Maybe not the best sister in the *world*.

"Or we take turns spendin' time with Teddy and Isab—"

"No, no, no, and no," she sang. "Here's what's gonna happen. Tomorrow after work, when Sebastian and I head down to Seattle, I'll tell him you're back in town. And once he's done throwin' a fit, I'll remind him of what I'm telling you right now. Teddy's only home from Thursday nights to Sunday afternoons for another two months, so those days are sacred. Those days are reserved for family, starting with pizza as soon as we're back in town around seven thirty. It's a new tradition we created when he started the program. Because Friday disappears— Teddy's in school and wants to catch up with his friends basically until he passes out. Sunday's gone too, 'cause it's all laundry and packing and driving him back down to Seattle."

As she took a breath, I put my hand on her arm, slowing her down.

"I get it," I said. She didn't need to explain further. I could see how this was taking its toll on her. She hated not having Teddy around every day. The last thing she needed was a conflict between her brother and best friend. "We'll suck it up in front of Teddy. That's a promise."

Somehow.

A voice in the back of my head was ready to scream out in terror, but this was the deal. After dragging things out as slowly as possible, shit was suddenly gonna be in motion. I'd see him tomorrow. *Fuck me.* My mouth became dry just thinking about it.

"Thank you. That means..." Soph trailed off when a set of headlights flashed over the trees to the left of us, and we looked over toward the street. "I think that's Dylan."

I crammed the last of my hot dog into my mouth and washed it down with a big gulp of beer, then rose to my feet. "Do you mind getting my sneakers in the back of the truck? They should be right at the front."

"Sure thing." She threw up the hood on her jacket and jogged out into the rain. Thankfully, it was back to drizzling.

In the meantime, I did my best to towel off my feet.

When Soph returned, I was distracted by the RV that appeared behind her. Maybe a neighbor was turning around at the end of the street. Either way, it couldn't be Dylan.

"False alarm," I said, nodding behind her.

She glanced over her shoulder, only to flash me a grin. "No, that's him."

I felt my forehead wrinkle with confusion.

"Do you remember what he does for a living?" she asked, tossing me my shoes.

"Uh..." Vaguely. "Something with engineering." Like me, Dylan was a college dropout. Three semesters for me, four for him. He'd studied technical engineering but walked away when his younger brother was diagnosed with cancer. The brother was fine today, but Dylan never went back to school. He'd found a job in town and worked his way up without a degree. I just didn't recall the specifics.

"They design and manufacture luxury features for campers, RVs, and those cute tiny homes," Soph reminded me.

"Ah. There's nothing cute about those homes," I felt the need to say.

"You're wrong, but whatever."

Easy for her to say; she was like five foot two. I used her head as an armrest just to prove my point, to which she batted it away and elbowed me in the ribs.

"Oof." I winced and held my side.

We watched Dylan pull over to the side of the property, right in front of the trees, and it was a grand vehicle. Looked like a brand-new RV. Winnebago, to be accurate. Mercedes chassis —probably one of those Sprinters. They were popular for RVs and camper vans. I'd rather live in one of those than a tiny home, that was for sure.

"So what am I missin' here?" I asked. "Are we camping together?"

Soph grinned.

Dylan opened the door and jumped out. "Beats the truck tent, doesn't it? It's yours for the next three weeks if you want."

Hot dang, for real? After quickly putting on my shoes, I walked over to him and inspected the RV. "Man, this is too much. It looks new—and my work here will be dirty."

"Don't worry about it." He waved that off. "I actually chose this one because it's got vinyl flooring instead of carpet. Roomier shower too. It's part of our retirement package—geared toward customers who want to travel comfortably as they get older."

"That's you, Blake!" Soph exclaimed.

I snorted in amusement.

"I cleared it with my boss and everything," Dylan went on.

"All we have to do is give it a field test, and then we can include my patio feature in the spring catalogue."

"What feature?" Soph and I asked in unison, and she jogged over to us.

Dylan smiled and showed us. He dove into an explanation too, one that revealed the love he had for his job. Basically, they had several RVs and campers in a showroom down at Cedar Point—no idea where that was—and it was how they put their designs on display. So this RV, for instance, had a built-in patio and an awning. Dylan flipped open a small hatch near the door and pressed a button.

I wasn't easily impressed, but Dylan got me there. I folded my arms over my chest and watched as an extension to the side of the RV unfolded before us. He spoke of experimenting with different supplies at work, constantly pushing light materials and durability closer to one another.

Four legs unfolded too, and the ends couldn't drill into the mud. Dylan had taken the ground into consideration in his design. The feet flattened and widened with a layer of some metal board before the mechanical whirring came to a stop.

"The awning's mechanical too," he said. "You'll find the remote for it inside the RV."

"This is goddamn impressive." I squatted down and gripped the edge of the patio, testing its flexibility. It certainly felt sturdy.

"My man's a genius," Soph gushed. "You two can probably discuss the structure of this thing for hours, but I'm cold and... Are we walking from here? Where's our car?"

She wasn't wrong. I loved these things. When construction met engineering, magic happened.

"Max has it. He's parked up the street," Dylan answered. "I figured that's what interns are for. We'll just drop him off on the way home." As I straightened again, he threw me the keys. "Can

I come over tomorrow around lunch and get some details on the building process? I feel a little lost."

"Of course. I'll be here. I can forward the plans and the blueprints too." I held up the keys. "I'll take good care of her."

"I'm not worried. Assuming you two have worked things out, I'll say it's good to have you back." He clapped me on my arm and grabbed Soph's hand.

"We did," she confirmed with a smile. "Let's go pick up our girl. And you can let your doggies out of the truck, Blake. I didn't even see Rosie. Is she still in Georgia?"

Aw, hell.

CHAPTER
4

I woke up well rested but with a rock in the pit of my stomach.

A glance at the clock started the internal countdown. Twelve hours and fourteen minutes till I saw Sebastian again for the first time since I'd split without a word.

It shouldn't fucking matter. At all. We'd shared a couple weeks together, and now, even after two months apart, he was still on my mind. How the fuck did that work? If that wasn't toxic, I didn't know what was.

Who knew how many guys he'd banged since then.

Ouch.

I ran a hand through my hair and glanced around me. Oppy and Percy were sprawled out on the floor by the door, clearly not in any rush this morning.

It was a nice RV. Spacious. Rather than one sleeping section in the back, resulting in a cramped seating area, it was just one big room and a small bathroom. One generously sized sofa and two cushy chairs transformed into three individual beds, and the dining table could be stowed away along the wall. Plenty of space for storage in the overhead compartments too, and the sleeper above the cab had a divider curtain. Even the kitchen was cool. I'd lived in apartments with smaller kitchenettes.

I made quick work of putting away the bed, washing up, and getting dressed. For once, it wasn't raining outside. So while I let the boys do their thing in the yard, I brought all my shit from the truck into the RV. Then I hooked up the RV to the power at the property line so I didn't have to worry about draining the batteries.

Buying groceries came next, and I didn't have to bring Percy and Oppy with me. It felt good. Something that felt even better was the fact that I had a kitchen now. I could make my own coffee in the morning, cook my own food, and not worry about finding ice packs for my cooler.

On the way "home," I bought new shoes too. I needed a nicer pair of dress shoes that I could use for going out. Brown leather went with most things, from jeans to suit pants.

Nine hours and fifty-four minutes till dinner.

I filled the little fridge and freezer, the cupboards as well, and stowed away the food and treats I'd bought for the boys in a couple compartments.

Dylan stopped by around noon, and he didn't arrive empty-handed. Aside from two burgers and fries, he had a list of questions from Soph. Things she'd been too overwhelmed to think of last night.

It wasn't as cold today—go figure, now that I didn't have to sleep in the truck—so Dylan and I made use of the patio as we ate. With the camping chair as a table in front of us, I pulled up the blueprints and plans for the property on my laptop, and I answered the questions best I could.

"Bottom line, this is your future home," I said, biting into my burger. "I'll follow your lead. I'm just taking liberties with the guesthouse."

Dylan chuckled and picked up his soda. "Blake, a guesthouse hasn't existed even in our wildest dreams. You do what you want with it. This whole thing is still surreal to us. We stayed up last night and just... We couldn't process it."

I supposed this was a good time to address another one of Soph's issues, which didn't come with any direct inquiries so much as a rant of rhetorical questions. "How do you thank someone for a house? Is this actually happening? How many things can go wrong so I can prepare myself?"

It didn't escape my notice that "How can we accept this?" wasn't written in Soph's familiar, girlie scrawl. That one had to be from Dylan.

"Here's the thing, Dylan. Y'all can thank me for buying the lot and being one of the guys holding the shovel or mixin' the cement, but the rest—it ain't my money. I can't use it myself. I don't like the reason I got it—at the same time, fuck if I'm gonna give it back. I've earned every damn buck. Soph, too. I ain't the only one who's put in countless hours on that ranch. Growing up, we were all at it. School breaks, weekends, holidays. She worked there full time before she got out." I stuck a couple fries into my mouth. "And not a single paycheck to show for it. She didn't sneak around like David and I did either, nor did she push her luck with an expensive car or high-end fashion."

He nodded slowly and wiped his mouth with a napkin.

"You and Soph are also the two people I wanna call home base," I admitted. "More and more lately, I feel uprooted and unsettled, and it would be nice to have a place where I get the sense, you know—this is where my family lives. This is where I can come visit. This is where we'll celebrate Christmas and have Thanksgiving dinner." I paused, unable to ignore Sebastian in this topic. "I'm sure Sebastian feels the same." Because in a way, he and I were alike. We were both outsiders who were a part of Soph and Dylan's crew. Next, I pointed my burger at the land in front of us. "This is it, man. It won't just be a home to you, Soph, and the kids. It'll be the crime scene for future holidays and get-togethers. This is for all of us."

He cracked a little grin. "I cannot tell you how perfect that sounds to me."

Well, good. That was good.

I took another bite of my burger. "I hope you still feel that way when it turns out that the solar panels were a fucking waste in this sunless state and all you manage to power up with them is the indicator lamp on your stove."

He laughed at that—hard.

———

Twenty-seven minutes to go.

I blew out a nervous breath and leaned the shovel against the scaffolding.

The good thing about having a construction project to distract me was that hours could go by, wars could start, a zombie apocalypse could begin, and I wouldn't even notice. The bad part...well, I'd lost hours to taking measurements, digging a trench around the area that would support the guesthouse, and now I had less than half an hour to prepare myself to face Sebastian again.

The plans had changed too, which I wasn't too happy about. I'd seen the text from Soph last time I went in to get coffee, and it'd taken me a solid ten minutes to agree and confirm.

Pizza night had moved to right here. Sebastian wanted to "see the place with his own eyes."

After stowing away my tools, I ushered the boys back into the RV and closed the door. Then I brought out my last clean change of clothes before stripping out of today's work outfit. Everything went into a black trash bag. Tomorrow I would have to track down a laundromat.

I showered, brushed my teeth, but couldn't be assed to shave —as usual. The bathroom might be on the larger side of what I'd seen in RVs before, but it was still tiny to anyone over six feet.

Fourteen minutes left.

My stomach tightened further, and I hated it. It was the toxicity. How could Soph and David not understand? This was Sebastian's doing. He made me feel this crap.

How the fuck did that not mean he was bad news?

I shook my head to myself and put on a pair of boxer briefs, followed by jeans, socks, sneakers, belt, a black Henley, and my Bulldogs cap. My new shoes would have to wait until the outdoors wasn't so muddy—or until I had a date. I wanted to try that eventually. Definitely not with anyone who made me feel like an insecure teenager, but someone who was...nice. Someone who was okay.

"Anybody home?" I heard Dylan holler from outside.

My breath hitched a little before I reminded myself that Dylan was safe.

In fact, I was glad he arrived first.

Making sure the dogs stayed behind, I headed outside and spotted Dylan dragging something out of his car. Or a company car. I hurried over there to help him.

"I can't control the rain," he grunted, setting the heavy-looking heater on the ground. "But I can give you a heated patio."

"Buddy, that's unnecessary." I was just gonna use the grill to spread some warmth. I'd extended the awning earlier to provide extra shelter too.

"It's not just for you," he replied. He walked back to pop the trunk next. "You're out of your mind if you think you're gonna build the guesthouse on your own. Sebastian and I will help out —but we'll need a place to sit where we don't have to worry about bringing half the yard inside."

51

He had a point. But perhaps we could skip the part where Sebastian helped out. Dylan was plenty. He and I could set up a coffee break station on the patio, a notion that quickly grew on me. It would give me a chance to show my future brother-in-law that I was worth keeping around.

Dylan retrieved four foldable chairs and a matching table from the trunk and said it was part of the field test too. He was curious to see how much weight the patio could handle.

"Well, let me help," I said.

Dylan nodded at the car. "Isabella's asleep in her carrier. I'll grab this. You get reacquainted with your niece."

No complaints from me. I rounded the car and opened the door, and it was a precious fucking sight. Someone else would've thought so too. Rosie had always loved babies. We'd visited whenever David's wife popped out another young'un, and my girl would guard the newborn with her life.

"You're gonna love me more than you love Sebastian, li'l Bella." I unfastened her carrier and picked it up, praying I didn't wake her.

Between setting up the patio furniture, hooking up the heater, and turning the grill into the evening's bonfire, we'd lost the last of the daylight, Isabella woke up, and no sign of Soph, Sebastian, and Teddy.

Dylan came out from the RV after changing Isabella's diaper, and I decided that was a good time for me to carry her a little. She had to get to know me. Also, I had to begin her education in southern livin'. I sure as heck couldn't count on Soph to cover that part, because she was forgetting. It was a tragedy.

"First lesson, sugar," I said, cupping the back of her head and pressing a kiss to her cheek, "is music."

I picked a playlist on my phone and connected to the speakers, including the soundbar under the awning. Then I refocused on Isabella as the first notes of Elle King's "America's Sweetheart" poured out over the patio, and I admitted to my niece that I had a minor crush on the singer. She was ballsy and brazen and had a cool voice.

"Sebastian texted." Dylan sat down in one of the chairs. "They just left the pizza place, so they should be here in five."

"All right." I was getting the ab workout of the year in sheer nervousness. "I'm just gonna focus on you, little darlin'." I kissed Isabella's forehead and moved a bit to the music. With my hand behind her head, I held her away from me enough so I could get a look at her face, and she was a perfect mix of her mama and daddy. Big, beautiful eyes like Soph, dark hair from Dylan.

"You know what I find interesting?" Dylan asked. "You're a nervous wreck, and he's been so royally pissed—like I've never seen him. The way I see it, nothing about what you had was casual. Casual doesn't evoke that kind of—"

"The way *I* see it, Daddy Dylan should shut his trap," I cooed to Isabella. "Yes, he should."

My perfect niece cooed right back and grabbed on to my nose, and I couldn't help but grin at her.

"You like this music, don't you?" I rubbed my nose against hers and growled playfully. This was the best age. They didn't talk back, they didn't find adults embarrassing, and they didn't try to bail from birthday parties to go out with friends instead. They also didn't call you out for being a bad singer.

Isabella's eyes went wide with wonder, and she grabbed at me as I sang along with the tune, and then—and then she fucking laughed. Or squealed.

"Holy shit!" Dylan shot up from his chair and pulled out his phone. "Keep going, man. It's her first laugh!"

I didn't know whether to be insulted or fist-pump the air in triumph, but I went with it because the sound was amazing. So I kept singing along to the song, and I kept moving Isabella to the beat while she laughed and squeezed my nose.

Dylan filmed it and grinned like the proud daddy he was. "God—that sound. Let's see. October 17, our daughter's first laugh. Isabella, Daddy, and Uncle Blake on the grounds of what's going to be our home. Mommy, you better hurry."

Funnily enough, the headlights of a car flashed over the trees mere seconds later, and it kicked Dylan into motion. He jumped off the patio and darted toward the car.

It was a reprieve. I was with family. My nerves about Sebastian took a hike for a precious moment, and all that existed was this. Another milestone to add to my collection of firsts. I'd witnessed two of David's kids' first steps too, Lee-lee's first time singing solo at a school recital, and Joshua pulling out his first loose tooth in the barn behind their house.

"She's laughing, baby! Hurry! Teddy, you too—come on."

"Dad, I'm home!" I heard Teddy shout. Default mode for when he was excited.

Soph gasped at the same time. "Oh my God—are you sure? It could be gas."

"And it's so good to see you, son." Dylan gave Teddy a squeeze and ushered him toward us. "I'm sure, Soph. I swear—just listen to her."

A beat later, I was swarmed by family members, and my sister wrestled her way to my side while Teddy ran right up to me and wrapped his arms around my middle.

"I'm happy you're here again, Uncle Blake!"

The kid melted my heart.

A moment of commotion had to be untangled; Soph needed to know how to keep Isabella giggling, and Dylan and I spoke at once about what I'd done. Simultaneously, I handed over the little darling to Soph so I could hug my nephew.

"I'm even happier, Teddy, I'll tell you that." I squeezed him tightly and took him to the side for a semblance of privacy. "Lemme get a look at my champ."

He grinned up at me, and I cupped his cheeks.

"You gotta quit gettin' taller, ya hear?" I couldn't believe I'd lasted so long before I'd come crawling back. "Give me your game face."

He remembered, and it made my day. He flexed his muscles and growled like a mean killing machine, and I mirrored the pose and growled right back, much to his delight.

I pulled him in for another hug and kissed the top of his head. "I'm sorry for not saying goodbye when I left this summer, buddy."

He shrugged and ran his fingers along the ink on my arms. "I don't like saying goodbye. But Momma said you're staying longer now."

"Much, much longer," I promised. Someone moved in the corner of my eye, and I knew it was him. It was as if my body had a Sebastian radar, which was mildly terrifying. "I wanna hear all about that new school of yours. Are you making any new friends?"

"Four!" he boasted. "Right, Momma? I have four new friends!"

"Yes, you're quite the popular boy in Seattle, sweetie." Soph joined us with Isabella in her arms and combed her fingers through Teddy's hair. "Are we ready for pizza?"

Dammit. I was hoping to drag this out. I didn't wanna have to acknowledge Sebastian. By now, he was on the patio too, opening pizza boxes with Dylan.

"Yeah, come on—I'm starving," Dylan said. "Everyone sit down."

"I'll grab the drinks in the car." That was Sebastian. Hadn't heard his voice in two months, and...fuck. *Fuck.*

I lifted my gaze as he stepped off the patio and trailed

toward the car, and it caused a whirlwind of memories to resurface from this summer. He was...a *behemoth* of a man, and that was coming from me. I hadn't weighed below two hundred pounds since high school, and I couldn't exactly call myself short at six-one. And yet, he was larger. Everywhere.

When he turned it on, his personality was immense. He cracked jokes and was sweeter than sugar to Teddy, but Christ—I remembered when he finally reeled me in. The jokester was nowhere to be found. Rough didn't come close to describing it. He took, commanded, and beckoned. He turned me into a desperate fucking whore.

I could still see it in my head, my fantasies, my dreams. The muscles of his back rippling beneath my fingers, his biceps bulging, the veins in his forearms showing, his torso becoming defined as he pounded into me—

"Christ," I exhaled to myself.

In a way, Sebastian Wilder was the personification of deception, because I wouldn't have been able to guess what kind of man he was in the sack just by looking at him. I mean, sure, he was big. Probably around six-five, no exaggeration, stocky frame, solid strength. But he was also Teddy's personal clown, wore flip-flops in the summer, and had one of those man-buns.

My father would've looked him up and down, spat out some chew, and felt that all his preconceived notions about people from Washington were correct.

My first impression of Sebastian was nowhere near being accurate. I'd seen a hot-as-fuck man and thought, hey, maybe we could fuck. But in the end, it'd never been up to me. Once my intentions had been clear, he'd taken over completely. More than that, he'd shown me other sides to himself that were unforgettable.

Those were the sides that made him downright lethal.

Teddy wanted to sit between Sebastian and me, so I made my way to the table and sat down at the head. Sebastian returned shortly after, and no one wasted any time grabbing their first slice.

It was still weird for me to be part of a family dinner where no one said grace. It'd been the rule for as long as I'd lived. If dinner was among family and you sat at a table, someone said grace.

Fuckin' heathens up here.

I removed my ball cap and left it on my lap.

"Momma, can we live in an RV?" Teddy asked.

"You think we have too much space at home?" Soph smirked.

Teddy grinned sheepishly. "No, but we could go anywhere!"

I chuckled and grabbed myself a Coke.

"Where would all your toys go?" Dylan asked.

Teddy hadn't considered that. "Maybe in my room at Bastian's house?"

Sebastian shot him a little grin but didn't say anything. He was usually so vocal. Now, because I was here, shit was weird. He hadn't looked my way once. Not a glance as far as I knew.

I'd avoided looking at him since the moment they got here, but now that I was sitting so close to him, it seemed I couldn't look away. He was too fucking gorgeous. Stunning. Still so immense, yet with heaps of charm.

Isabella was getting fussy in Dylan's arms, and Soph said she couldn't put off feeding her any longer. She excused herself to head inside and nurse the little one.

"Don't step on Oppy and Percy, please," I said.

"Oh! I wanna see them, Uncle Blake!" Teddy pleaded and almost knocked back his chair when he stood up. As if I could deny him. "Momma, I go with you." He grabbed a new pizza slice and tumbled toward Soph.

Dylan turned a perturbed look Soph's way. "You're leaving me with those two?" He just didn't know how to whisper.

Soph thought that was hilarious and just giggled in response. Then she disappeared into the trailer with the kids, and the tension automatically turned awkward and agitated. The latter came from Sebastian, because without Teddy around, he didn't have to pretend.

"Are you gonna fucking eat or what?" Sebastian asked irritably.

I glanced at Dylan, who was in the middle of finishing a slice, and it dawned on me that the question was for me.

"Huh?" I managed. Wow, he was talking to *me*.

Sebastian flicked me an impatient look. "You've lost weight, and you're not eating. Are you sick or just dumber than you look?"

"This is nice," Dylan said. "We should do this more often."

I furrowed my brow and wondered what the hell Sebastian's problem was. Okay, I could venture a guess, but if he wanted to avoid me, avoid talking to me, he didn't have to worry about what I ate.

"I don't know what you're talkin' about—I haven't lost any weight."

"Dumber than you look, then. Because yeah, you have." He tossed a crust into one of the boxes and leaned back, his posture and expression saying he was letting it go. He didn't wanna talk anymore.

"So how are the Pugs doing, Blake?" Dylan interjected. "Or was it Bulldogs?"

I slid my stare to Dylan instead and let some humor seep in. Bless him. "You don't have to run interference, buddy. When

Sebastian's ready to hash things out like a real man, these passive-aggressive little bitch fits will be history."

"Boy, there's nothing passive about my aggression," Sebastian laughed. "Unlike that snide remark you just offered."

"What was that, baby? Yeah, I'll be right there." Dylan abruptly left his seat and fled inside.

Christ. We knew how to clear a room. Or a patio.

"We might as well get this out of the way so we can move on," Sebastian told me, and I lifted a brow, admittedly curious. "Soph told me you were building them a house, and it goes without saying that I will be here to help out whenever I can. But as far as I'm concerned, there's no reason you and I gotta talk. We'll act civil around Teddy, and then—" He shrugged. "I'll just wait until you run back into your closet in Georgia again."

Nice speech. He had it all figured out, huh?

I'd half expected Soph to tell him everything, including the part where I came out to my folks and got the boot. In retrospect, this made more sense. It was a personal topic—and my story to tell.

Not that it mattered. Sebastian clearly didn't want it, and truth be told, maybe it was for the best. My willpower and self-control didn't exist around this man, and I had to keep my distance, something that would be a lot easier if he didn't pity me or whatever.

"All right." I nodded with a dip of my chin. "I take it you're not interested in an apology for leaving the way I did."

He smiled faintly, a humorless twist of his lips that left me a few degrees colder. "No, you can save your excuses for someone who gives a rat's ass."

I wasn't gonna lie; that one stung. But I couldn't blame him. We'd shared something this summer, and I'd bailed in the most cowardly way. Like always.

At the same time, I couldn't help but feel irritated. He'd hurt me too, goddammit. He'd used his weird hippie voodoo on me. He'd given me anxiety and fears. He'd turned me into a headcase.

"Got it," I replied tightly.

CHAPTER
5

The longer I stayed in the RV, the more I enjoyed it. I could suddenly understand why some people sold off all their belongings and hit the road in one of these when they retired.

My most recent hobby was a new favorite. While Soph did laundry and prepared for Teddy's return to Seattle on Sundays, he spent that day with me in the RV. We sprawled out across my bed, a soda for him, a beer for me, a bag of chips between us, the boys nearby, and *Wicked Tuna* filled the little flat-screen attached to the cabinet in front of us.

"I wish my bed had a cupholder, Uncle Blake." Teddy returned his soda to the armrest.

"It's cool, innit?" I threw a handful of chips into my mouth and watched one of the fishermen on the show haul in a big-ass tuna. "We should go fishing in the spring, champ."

"Yes!" He made sure to mirror my pose. Feet crossed at the ankles, one arm behind his head, and pillow propped up *just so* underneath. It was cute. "We'll let the fishes go back in the water after, right?"

I side-eyed him. "Food's meant to be eaten, not played with."

He squinted at me. "I like fried fish. Bastian brings it home when he works at the restaurant. It's yummy with ketchup."

"There you go. If we catch fish, we can fry it."

"But Momma said I can't eat fried food a lot. It's not good for me." He stuck out his tongue at nothing, clearly not a fan of health talk.

"Unfortunately, your mama's right. But now that I'm in town, I'mma introduce you to so much amazing food that's not too unhealthy, you won't believe it. Did you know I'm the best cook in the family?"

He grinned. "Are you?"

"Damn right. I'll show you." Another thing to look forward to. I knew the struggles Teddy faced, as did others with Down syndrome, and I was itching to pull my weight. Sebastian already did a lot that focused on exercise and staying active.

I hadn't been active in sports since I'd played football in high school, so that wasn't where I shone. I was blessed with good genes and had always taken jobs that gave me a good work-out. Food, on the other hand, had become an involuntary passion over the years because of the different places I'd traveled to and the various jobs I'd tried. Not to mention the people I'd met along the way.

"You excited to go back to Seattle?" I asked.

"I miss Momma and Dad and Isabella and Bastian and you, but yeah." He nodded and welcomed Oppy to sprawl out on his stomach. "I like all my friends. And Ms. Nora gives me gold stars in my sticker book. I have so many."

That approach was definitely a winner with Teddy.

"I'm not surprised. You're my champ for a reason."

He smirked, showing the first signs of the future teenager in him. Only a year to go. He was coming home earlier next week, on Wednesday, since he turned twelve the day after.

Just as the episode ended on the screen, I heard the telltale sound of a vehicle pulling in nearby. The problem was, it didn't sound like Soph and Dylan's car.

Soph had warned me earlier when I picked up Teddy that Dylan might work overtime today, on a damn Sunday, in which case Sebastian would pick up the boy and drive him down to Seattle.

"I reckon we have a visitor, buddy." I got off the bed and picked up Percy, keeping him on my shoulder, and the bag of chips. A glance out the window revealed Sebastian climbing off his four-wheeler.

Goddammit.

I'd seen him almost every day lately, and it hadn't gotten easier. He'd worked in construction a lot too, so the man knew what he was doing. We could work on the guesthouse side by side for hours and only exchange brief strings of conversation— strictly related to what we were doing.

The man could hold a grudge.

I opened the door and stuck my hand into the chips, retrieving a handful. I was mildly obsessed with Ruffles. "I take it Dylan's workin' late."

Sebastian eyed me, or mainly Percy, and nodded with a dip of his chin. "Mind if I borrow your truck? Their car is acting up."

I made a mental note to head over there tomorrow and take a look at it. "Just don't wreck it." I grabbed the key from the kitchen counter and tossed it to him. "Teddy, Shrek is here to see you."

Sebastian rolled his eyes.

Teddy already knew who it was, so he bounded over and hollered, "Bastian! I see you!"

Funny how quickly that put a gorgeous smile on Sebastian's mug. Man, I loathed how fucking sexy he was. Especially when he smiled like that.

"I see you too, little man." Sebastian stepped closer and told the boy to get his things. It was time to get on the road. While

Teddy returned to the bed to put his coloring book and farm animal play set into his backpack, Sebastian addressed me again. "My boss at the restaurant is out of town, so I'll be working there most nights this week and the next. If you want, I can come over tomorrow morning and help you finish the exterior."

That would be too much work for him. "Even Shrek needs some downtime. All I gotta do tomorrow is finish the roof and attach gutters." I had an electrician and a plumber coming on Tuesday, so I wouldn't need Sebastian then either. "If you can spare a few hours on Wednesday, we could get the interior wall sections up—I can do the rest myself."

It'd been a rough ten days, but I'd be a liar if I said Sebastian—and Dylan—hadn't made the work easier. The hardest part was over. The guesthouse sat on a solid foundation, the exterior looked really fucking good with a couple coats of white paint, everything was insulated to perfection, and the framework was real sturdy. Now waited the interior, which was a one-man job once the kitchenette and bathroom were installed.

Sebastian cocked his head. "Did you lay the floor already?"

I nodded and caught Percy, who was about to slide off my shoulder. "Last night. I had to get it done before the electrician and plumber arrive, and I didn't wanna be swamped tomorrow."

I wasn't gonna be good company on Wednesday, because it was Rosie's birthday. Luckily for me, Sebastian wasn't looking for good company.

"Fair enough. Wednesday—I can be here at nine." He reached out and cupped his hand over Percy's head. "You were right about one thing. Your Yorkie mutts are adorable as fuck. Too bad their daddy is a complete piece of shit."

It was a punch straight to the gut. Heating me up just a little bit with his love for animals, then ripping the rug out from underneath and striking me with an ice-cold fist. My face fell, and I didn't have the energy to hit back. I was suddenly wrung-out and felt entirely too vulnerable.

I took a step back as Teddy reappeared, none the wiser, with a happy smile on his face.

I didn't know why I was here. Of all the places I could go to get wasted, I was parked in the marina's lot, seconds away from Quinn's Fish Camp on the boardwalk where Sebastian was working.

Perhaps I wanted him to finish the job. I felt like shit, and I couldn't pretend it was only because of Rosie. Lately, too much had been building up inside me. Losing Rosie, the rejection of my parents, the way Sebastian acted toward me, feeling so damn uprooted... I'd declined a dinner invitation at Soph and Dylan's for Teddy's homecoming today; I'd see him tomorrow for his birthday, and I needed that time to get my shit together. But I didn't wanna be completely alone tonight either. Even if that meant showing up at Sebastian's work and facing more biting comments about what a piece of shit I was.

He hadn't said anything today, though. In fact, he'd been extra quiet.

I climbed out of my truck and adjusted my Stetson. Being down in the dumps was no excuse to look like a slob. I'd shined my new shoes too, and I'd bought a black button-down because my other shirts needed to be ironed.

As I headed toward the boardwalk, I could see through the windows of the restaurant that it was divided into two sections. Seemed like the dinner guests ate in one part, and then there was a bar in the other where the tables stood closer to one another. I spotted fishnets and old glass floats hanging from the ceiling, and a skipper's wheel graced the back of the bar.

I opened the door and was met by soft country rock and the scents of grilled fish, spices, and oak. It took no time at all to locate Sebastian because he was right there behind the bar, pouring beer.

Wednesday night wasn't the busiest this place had seen, I was guessing. I counted about a dozen people in this area, including the four who sat at the bar.

I sidestepped and held the door open as two women headed out with to-go boxes. Only, one of them tripped on the carpet, and I hurriedly reached out and righted her.

"You okay, ma'am?"

"Wow," she laughed breathily, a flush spreading on her cheeks. "Uh, yeah. Thank you."

I dipped the brim of my hat and let her go.

Sebastian was looking at me when I turned my attention to finding a seat, and I figured the end of the bar would be a good spot for me tonight. It was a little more secluded, and the man who clearly wasn't happy about seeing me would be able to ignore me easier if I sat in the corner.

He met me there on his side of the bar when I slid onto a stool.

"Were all the other places in town full?" he asked.

"I already know I'm not welcome here, but thank you for the reminder." I nodded at the shelf. "I'd like two shots of tequila and whatever dark lager you have on tap." I pulled out my wallet from the back pocket of my jeans and requested to start a tab too.

They appeared to have a good selection of beers and liquor here. That boded well for me.

Sebastian furrowed his brow, as if he was trying to read me, but I was empty tonight. Or rather, I was a book he didn't wanna open. It wasn't pretty inside.

"Any preference on the tequila?"

I shook my head and shrugged out of my jacket. Tonight I'd drink cat piss if it got me wasted.

He returned with my drinks a hot minute later, and I wasted no time.

Happy birthday, sugar. I miss you.

I threw back the first shot and grimaced at the intense flavor. The second shot went down as quickly, and then I took a swig of my beer. Shouldn't be too long now before the numbness set in.

Sebastian kept busy, glancing my way every now and then, and I buried myself in my phone to avoid the looks. I scrolled through pictures of Rosie and the boys, and I realized, for the longest time, my dogs had been the only constant that didn't make me wanna chase that numbness. In every other aspect of my life, I'd played things safe for as long as I could remember.

I could be the center of attention at a party one night, only to slide out the back door when the sun rose and never go back to that place again. Never see those faces again.

Noticing that my beer was gone, I set my phone on the bartop and lifted my gaze. A couple had left, a few more had arrived. Sebastian was at the other end of the bar, and the guy he was talking to looked a little too interested.

I narrowed my eyes.

"Bartender," I hollered.

Sebastian exchanged a couple more words, perhaps telling the guy he'd be right back—what the fuck did I know—and then he made his way back to me.

"Another beer, please," I requested. "Wouldn't mind a nice bourbon either."

"All right."

I watched him work. I watched his forearms and his hands as he picked a bourbon from the top shelf, how he poured it into a glass, and then how he grabbed a new beer glass from under the counter and walked over to the nearest tap. This was mindless work, and he made it look easy. Graceful, almost. Being a bartender wasn't his passion in life, so he probably didn't go the extra mile to know a million cocktail recipes, but whenever someone gave him a job to do, he did it well.

When he handed me my drinks, he also removed the empty glasses, and then he was gone again. The fucker returned to that other guy, and either they were flirting or they knew each other well enough to sport grins and slip back into conversation as if they'd done it many times before.

The bourbon became a soothing medicine to fight the bitterness that flowed through me.

This was his fucking fault. Sebastian had made me feel too much. He'd shattered a wall of detachment around me and brought me out to where life hurt you.

How far would he go with me around? If that guy leaned forward, would Sebastian go for it? Fuck, I could see it in my head. I could see how they both leaned in and met in a kiss over the bar.

Jealousy and nausea churned in my stomach.

Maybe I'd see the moment Sebastian slipped him the tongue too.

Motherfucker.

Anger started brewing under the surface.

I swallowed the rest of my bourbon and let it trail heat down my throat. "Bartender."

Sebastian straightened and came my way once more, the smile he'd had for his new man gone. On the way, he removed a couple glasses from the bar.

"Gimme a drink," I said. "Maybe something that takes an hour to mix."

Sebastian's forehead creased. "Is this your dinner? It's a little soon for you to be lit already."

"I ain't lit. Just quit keepin' tabs on what I eat and do your job." I pushed the empty glass across the bar and grabbed my beer. "You can talk to your new boyfriend over there after you've clocked out."

They could go on Sebastian's goddamn four-wheeler and move the party to his beach house. To his bed.

Fuckers.

Sebastian became stone-faced and picked a bottle of vermouth from the shelves. "Since when do you care about who I see?"

"I fucking don't." I chugged half my beer and wondered why the hell he was bringing out a martini glass. Did I look like a martini guy? "Better him than me. Hell—if anythin', I feel sorry for the guy."

Who didn't stand a chance. He was gonna fall victim to Sebastian's hippie voodoo next, and he'd become an anxiety-ridden mess of emotions and doubts. I knew what I was talking about.

Sebastian set the glass in front of me with a little too much force, then dropped a cocktail onion in it before stalking away.

"I'm not a martini guy!" I called.

"It's not a martini." This time, he didn't stop walking. He left the area altogether, and another guy appeared seconds later.

He had the same kind of T-shirt, black, with the restaurant's logo in small print, but he didn't wear it like Sebastian did. The fabric didn't stretch around this guy's biceps.

I took a sip of my non-martini and thought it tasted an awful lot like a martini.

It wasn't bad.

———

Sebastian came back two drinks later. His date had left by then.

The dinner crowd was thinning out, and they didn't seat

any new guests. Around that time, the music was cranked up to place focus on the bar crowd, which had evidently grown while I'd guzzled booze.

It didn't escape my attention that the other bartender was sticking around, and I had a feeling Sebastian chose the other half of the bar as his territory for a reason.

And it was just perfect. It was what people in my life did— they distanced themselves from me.

"Hey, is that a real cowboy hat?" someone asked.

I tilted my head toward the three women sitting closest to me, about six feet up the bar.

"I think so," I replied. "It doesn't feel pretend anyway."

"Ohh, he's an actual Southerner," one of them gushed. Alcohol had a way of making someone think they were whispering when they weren't.

The middle one, clearly the one who'd had the most drinks, spoke next. "Do you work on a farm?"

I furrowed my brow. "Ma'am, I'm a rancher."

Or I used to be. Fuck. I drained the last of my drink and flagged down the bartender.

As he leaned close, I asked, "Can you get me Sebastian?"

"Sure, man."

I was an idiot. This wasn't how I avoided that man.

Sebastian had reluctance written all over him but came over anyway. "There's nothing in this bar I can give you that he can't."

I could think of a couple things, but I wasn't going to.

"Liquor me up, darlin'. I could go for somethin' simple now. Rum and Coke."

He held out his hand. "If you give me your car keys."

What did he take me for? I wasn't driving home in this condition. I was raised to sleep it off in my truck.

"I wasn't gonna drive," I muttered defensively, digging out

my keys. I dropped them into his hand, and he pocketed them. "Wait—" What the fuck was wrong with me? "Why did I just agree to that?"

That earned me a chuckled huff, and it was the warmest response I'd gotten from him since I'd left.

As he got crackin' on my drink, I couldn't resist watching him again. A few drinks made me more honest with myself, which I supposed wasn't good, but... The truth had a time and place too. And the truth was, I'd never been so happy as I'd been this summer. That was what hurt so damn much. He'd shown me a glimpse of what it could be like.

When I hadn't been busy fearing the inevitable end of my visit, life had been so good. Sebastian had made me feel alive. Really alive.

My God, I missed being oblivious. Because he'd been dead set on never crossing any lines either. I'd gotten what I wanted, a fling with an expiration date.

I scrubbed a hand over my face, unable to stick with one feeling. Was I pissed at him? Did I miss him? Was I pining? Did I wanna punch him in the fucking throat for causing me pain? Did I regret anything?

He set a rum and Coke in front of me, and I adjusted my hat by the crown and felt more confused than ever.

"I thought cowboys weren't allowed to wear their hats indoors," Sebastian said.

"There're exceptions." I waved that off and took a swig of the drink. It was good. Strong. Fuck, perfect. "You know what? You're a rum and Coke. Strong and biting, a certain hangover—a real bad one—but with enough sweetness that you keep comin' back for more. You don't understand the damage until it's done —until you're in shreds."

Sebastian rested his hands on the bartop and tilted his head at me. "Are you in shreds, Blake?"

I laughed, kinda hard, and held out my arms. "Ain't that obvious, darlin'? I'm so desperate to belong somewhere that I show up in a place where no one can't stand me."

Not unlike back home. No one could stand me there either.

"Fuck." My humor died, and it felt like my stomach was sucked into a black void, taking my smile and my composure with it. I had to get away. As I hauled out my wallet, I finished my drink in four gulps. "Lemme pay and get outta here. The tab —close it."

I shouldn't have had that last...two drinks and... I'd lost count of the beers.

On the flip side, I could no longer focus on anybody's face, because everyone was moving too fast.

He returned with a receipt for me to sign, and I scribbled a reasonable amount for a tip, I was pretty sure. Then I slipped off the seat and almost stumbled back, but I managed to grab on to the edge of the bar.

"Wait by your truck," Sebastian instructed. "I'll take you home."

No. Christ—no. I had to get away from him. I shook my head and shrugged into my jacket. "Leave it. I'll walk." With a two-finger wave, I left the corner of the bar and headed outside.

Jesus. Walking wasn't as easy as some people believed.

The cold air hit me as I stepped outside, and it wasn't entirely unwelcome. Now I just had to take a piss. Barely any people around, so that was nice. Like my life. Fuckin' empty. Oh, now I was really hosting a pity party for myself. Boardwalk empty, pier empty, marina empty, parking lot... The parking lot was closest. Unless I was gonna take a leak on someone's restaurant window, and it'd been a while since I'd sunk that low.

The parking lot was framed by bushes that hadn't lost all their leaves yet, so that was where I unbuckled my belt and unzipped my pants.

Glancing up at the night sky, I let out a breath that misted in the air.

Stars were out. Some clouds too.

"Blake!"

Aw, man.

"I'm'n the li'l boys' room!" I yelled back.

By the time Sebastian reached the parking lot, I was zipped up again and struggling with my belt. Fuckin' piece of...

"Who the fuck needs belts anyway." I gave up, annoyed and impatient. "What do you want?" I asked him. "I don't wanna hear any more shit. Drunks have feelings too—and we produce more stars." I gestured toward the sky. "I bet I can see more than you can."

His mouth twitched, but I didn't know if it was his I'm-trying-not-to-laugh-at-you-boy kind of amusement or the evil little hint of a smirk that said he wanted to bash my head in. To be frank, it looked like a combination of both.

"Go back to work," I urged. Then I draped my arms along the side of the bed of my truck behind me. "I'll wait here by my truck until I'm sober enough to walk home."

Had I grown taller tonight? It felt like it.

Sebastian pointed at my truck. "That's not yours."

"Huh?" I turned around and— "I'll be damned." Good thing I didn't try to open the door. Mystery solved, too. No wonder I felt taller; this truck wasn't as big as mine.

"Come on. I'll take you home." He nodded toward what I assumed was my actual truck.

Only a dozen or so cars remained in the parking lot that easily had room for forty or fifty, and I found my baby parked next to a rusty Corolla.

"Just gimme the keys," I said. "I mean it—I'll stay here for a while."

I didn't wanna breathe the same air as him right now. He

was too hot, and I was drunk enough to push buttons I should steer clear of.

"Or you can stop being so fucking difficult and get in the damn truck," he replied irritably. "You've been testing my patience all goddamn night, and I'm done. I'm driving you home, end of discussion."

Something inside me snapped, and I couldn't control it. Anger unfurled within me and caused me to implode so hard that my next breath hurt. He was done? No, *I* was done. I was fucking done being the bad guy all the fucking time.

"What part of gimme the keys do you not understand?" I demanded.

He shot me a glare. "I'm not having this argument when you're three sheets to the wind. Get in the fucking truck—you gotta walk your dogs anyway. You have to get home."

"And I told you I'll walk!" I yelled. Now he was criticizing me as a dog owner too. He thought I didn't know when my boys needed to go out? Screw him.

"I swear to Christ—" He cursed under this breath, then made a move to grab my arm.

I was having none of it. I ducked his hand, only to return and shove him away from me. He stumbled back, momentarily stunned I'd packed any strength at all, but then my element of surprise was gone. He came at me again, angrier than before, and slammed me up against my truck.

I groaned at the impact, and the pain spread down my spine. It made me fucking boil.

"I'm not telling you again," he seethed. The telltale sound of my car alarm being deactivated reached my ears, followed by him ripping open the passenger side's door. "*Get in.*"

"Fuck you," I rasped. I summoned all the anger I had and managed to punch him in the jaw, to which he quickly countered with a fist to my stomach.

Oh God. I coughed and bowled over, dropping my hat in the process.

Sebastian wasn't finished with me yet. He grabbed me by my shoulders and rammed me against the truck once more, and he leaned close. "I quit," he gritted out. "Get lost on your way home and choke on your vomit for all I care. I'm *done.*"

Now he was finished with me.

Something pierced through me, like a sense of alarm or panic, but it pushed me forward as if I was driven by rage. Except, I didn't get far. Just as I planted an arm across his chest, I caught the wild fury in his eyes, and it disarmed me. So did the close proximity and a whiff of his cologne.

I tried and fucking tried to shove him back. My body refused. It was busy registering all the places we were touching. A slow rush of heat made its way through me, and I swallowed against the dryness in my throat and dropped my gaze to his lips.

Maybe it was an act of desperation. Maybe bitterness and jealousy from before—with that other guy. Maybe I'd just lost my last shred of sanity.

Ignoring the evident anger in his posture, I closed the distance and kissed him.

He went rigid. His hands came to my arms, and I knew he was a fraction of a second away from either pushing me back or drop-kicking me. So I let weeks of anguish take the wheel, and I poured myself into the kiss. I locked an arm around his neck and pleaded silently. I needed one moment. *Please don't fucking reject me tonight.* I couldn't take it.

Goose bumps rose all over, and a hungry sound escaped me when I felt his hand on my cheek. The relief that welled up as he tentatively kissed me back—I couldn't describe it.

He changed the air around us when he went all in and took charge. My back hit the truck once more, but no one was throwing punches this time. He shifted his hands to my jaw, then slid his fingers back to my neck and up into my hair as he angled me for a deep, demanding kiss.

For fear I'd startle him out of a decision he was undoubtedly going to regret, I made sure not to make another sound. I followed him instead, easily sinking into the pace he set, the rhythm he controlled. Every time he swept his tongue alongside mine, I had to swallow a moan. He brought me back to this summer and to all the moments he'd used my body like the fucking expert he was. He knew exactly which buttons to push and how to turn me into a pleading whore.

Life became good again. This was the hit I'd come back for throughout my stay this summer. When we were together, I wasn't anxious.

I let my hands roam his chest and back, feeling his muscles underneath my fingertips. His tee was in the way. Fuck, we were in the wrong place altogether. I wanted his bed, I wanted him working me relentlessly and repeatedly, I wanted bruises and marks.

As we made out, I got rid of my jacket and threw it onto the passenger's seat.

He drew a ragged breath and kissed his way down my neck. At the same time, I squeezed his ass to me, pressing his hard cock against my own. I couldn't help but moan. Sparks of desire shot through me, and—

"You're wasted," he said, breathing heavily.

Fuck. He couldn't back down.

"I can still list all the presidents and about a hundred reasons why me bendin' over for you is a good idea."

He groaned and kissed me again, brutally hard, and it was easy to tell he was warring with himself.

"We were never a good idea, Blake."

That pissed me off. He wanted me too—he couldn't fucking

deny it. Hell, I could prove it. I looked him dead in the eye and started unbuttoning his jeans.

"Yet, here you are," I said. "You'd rather drill into my ass than go home to your new boyfriend."

His eyes flashed with anger. "Some of us have morals. If I was in an exclusive relationship, I wouldn't be here with you."

"But there's *something* going on between y'all." I dared him to say I was wrong.

He chuckled darkly and batted away my hands. Then he spun me around, trapped me against the truck, and shoved down my jeans. A breath hitched in my throat.

"You wanna know the truth?" He spoke through gritted teeth and kicked my knees apart. "He asked me out a few weeks ago."

Son of a bitch, I fucking knew it. Another rush of jealousy flooded me, and it tripped me up. My heart pounded, my skin was hypersensitive, and the urgency within me blazed like wildfire.

The sound of a condom wrapper being torn invaded my ears.

"We went out for beers," he went on. "He asked me all the right questions, showed interest in the Quad and what I do..."

I gnashed my teeth, hating every word that came out of his mouth. But I had to hear them. I had to know.

Sebastian stepped closer, and the second his fingers brushed over my asshole, my knees threatened to cave. *Holy fuck.* He didn't wait around, nor was he gentle. He pushed the head of his cock between my ass cheeks, then forced himself all the way in. Pain exploded inside me, knocking the air out of my lungs, but his groan of sheer pleasure caused a reaction no amount of pain could top. He pressed his face to my neck and sank his teeth into my flesh, and all I felt was heat. Liquid heat.

"What was it you said—better him than you?" He nipped at

my ear, sharply enough to make me hiss. "Did you mean that? Do you wanna hear how hard I fucked him? How amazing it felt when he gagged around my cock?"

"No," I choked out. The hurt blinded me—or maybe it was the rage. "Tell me you didn't, you rat bastard."

"I didn't," he grunted and pulled out. "Halfway through dinner, I knew I wasn't even gonna be able to pretend."

Oh God.

Thank you.

The relief washed over me just as he pushed in again, and I took it. I took it gladly. Every punishing thrust, every anger-laden grab. I welcomed it all.

"I told him I wasn't ready for anything other than friendship," he said, out of breath. "But I hope I will be, because chasing mistakes with you will be the end of me." With that said, he grabbed me by my neck, shoved my upper body into the passenger's side, and I just barely managed to plant my hands on the seat.

He started fucking me harder and harder, making it impossible for me to speak. *I'm not a mistake*, I wanted to yell at him, but I lacked the confidence to sound believable.

If this was all I got, I was gonna make the most of it.

I squeezed my cock and closed my eyes, pretending everything was only going to get better from here. When I woke up tomorrow, I wouldn't be his enemy any longer.

Skin-on-skin contact seemed to work the best. He slipped a hand under my shirt and rubbed my back, then around my side to my stomach and chest, and it became everything. Hundred times more intimate than the hatefuck itself. I felt his forehead landing on my spine too.

I stroked my cock faster and focused on his hand, on his fingers brushing over the trail of hair leading from my belly button.

"Oh fuck," I breathed, eyes flashing open. He hit that spot within me, rubbed the head of his cock against it, and sent bolts of euphoria through my body. "Sebastian—"

"I know. I'll get you there."

I didn't doubt him. He knew exactly how to use the fiery pain to strengthen the pleasure. He went all in and touched me perfectly, seduced me, and replaced the cold reality with a warm fantasy.

I moaned as he raked his blunt fingernails along my chest.

"Still too damn beautiful for words." His voice came out labored and raw, and it pushed me closer to the edge. Especially when he said things like that.

The rhythm seduced me as much as he did. It was both brutal and intoxicating, almost forcing my impending release out of me. It shut down my filters too. I gasped and moaned and fucking begged, and it spurred him on just like it had this summer. He did love it when I begged.

"Only a whore like you would drop your pants in a parking lot," he grunted. "You don't even care if someone walks by."

Those words got me going. I started panting, and I screwed my eyes shut and surrendered to the final stretch. My body tingled, little bursts of need firing from one pleasure point to another and dropping lower and lower.

"You turned me into this," I moaned.

Seconds later, my orgasm rushed through me. I couldn't breathe or move. I tensed up all over, and ropes of come rushed out of my cock. It caused me to clamp down around Sebastian, and the reward was instant.

He groaned and scraped his teeth along my back, his body going rigid and his arms squeezing me tightly to him. It made me curse the damn rubber. Why did he even wear it? We'd fucked raw before. Did he think I'd been with others?

I shuddered violently as the aftershocks of the release shook me. Combined with Sebastian's cock throbbing in my ass, I was given a moment where all was well with the world.

The silence that followed was less wonderful. It was reality knocking on the door, and I wasn't sure I could go back to before. I didn't want to fight. I didn't want any more comments on what a dick I was.

Once he'd backed away from me, I did damage control and grimaced when I saw I'd blown my load on the side of the seat. That was gonna be fun to clean up tomorrow. Actually, I wanted to get it done right away, so I grabbed a pack of wipes from the glove box.

Sebastian found that funny.

I let him have it because I loved that sound. It'd been a long time since I'd heard him laugh. Or chuckle, I guessed. A laugh would be asking too much.

After zipping up and getting rid of our waste, I picked up my hat from the ground and brushed away some dirt.

"Can I drive you home now?" he asked.

I nodded once.

CHAPTER
6

"Do you think you can handle Teddy's birthday breakfast tomorrow?"

"Of course." I frowned at him. "Quit tryna get rid of me."

He rolled his eyes and made a turn. In this area, it was one residential neighborhood after another. "I'm not. I figured you're gonna be hungover."

"I'll be fine." I glanced out the window again and traced some stray raindrops on the glass with my finger. "Is that another tradition of yours? First the breakfast, then the party later in the day?"

"Not really," he answered. "Teddy always chooses an activity instead of a party, so we do the breakfast at my place because there's more room. We eat, he gets presents, and we have cake. Didn't you get Soph's text?"

Yeah, I should've paid more attention to the details. I remembered seeing something about breakfast at Sebastian's house at nine and then something about bowling.

"I'll read the fine print about the bowling tomorrow," I replied, adjusting in my seat. Damn, I was gonna be sore in the morning. "My ass hurts."

Sebastian laughed through his nose. "Good."

Dick.

"My heart hurts too, you know. Some compassion wouldn't kill you. I just lost my dog." My jaw ticked, and I had to take a breath to let the annoyance simmer down.

"What? Did Rosie die?" His posture changed, and I could've sworn I saw concern in his eyes for a brief moment. "I assumed she stayed behind in Georgia."

I shook my head. "I was gonna bring her, but I visited my brother on the way, and he has a knack for finding cancer in my dogs. Aggressive lymphoma—I had to put her down."

As much as it pained me, it felt kind of good to talk about it.

"Shit. I'm sorry, Blake. I know she meant the world to you."

I swallowed at a sudden onslaught of emotion and nodded with a dip of my chin. I was a little surprised he remembered her name, to be honest.

"She would've turned eleven today," I admitted. "Hence the wise decision to go get drunk."

"Ah." He nodded slowly and checked his blind spot before crossing Emsworth. In my research of the area, this was the road Realtors kept track of. It was more expensive to live within the area encased by Emsworth because it was closer to the marina.

People cared about the weirdest shit. A plot of land, if there'd actually been any, inside that area would've gone for three times as much as I paid for Soph and Dylan's. It was a matter of ten fucking minutes.

Case in point, we arrived at the end of Marten Lane way too fast.

In ten minutes, you couldn't even go from one end of our land in Georgia to the other.

Sebastian killed the engine on the street, as opposed to driving it onto the lot, and I realized he'd have to return to the marina somehow.

"I can ask Soph and Dylan to come get me in the mornin'," I said.

He raked his teeth over his bottom lip and glanced at the RV. "Or I can come get you. I gotta step out to buy juice and Nutella anyway. Teddy's list was very specific."

That coaxed a smile out of me. "All right. What time do you want me to be ready?" Luckily for me, I'd already wrapped Teddy's gifts. I just needed a shower and possibly the hair of the dog. We'd see how I felt. Most of the time, my hangover symptoms consisted of an insane thirst for water, pineapple juice, and coffee.

"I'll knock on the door to your mansion at seven thirty," he replied. "And that was a joke. I won't knock, so you better get your ass out here."

"Can't stop thinkin' of my ass, huh?"

He snorted and side-eyed me. "Get outta the truck, Kidd."

"Okay, Wilder," I mocked and opened the door. I was starting to think he loved my truck. "For the record, that is a mansion to me. Just imagine being able to hit the road whenever you want—and you don't even have to leave your home. You could be walking Mischa and Echo in Redwood tomorrow."

He was watching me as I jumped out of the truck and turned to face him.

"Never settle down, split when you want to. Yeah, that sounds like you."

Oh, for fuck's sake. "That's gettin' old. I have heaps of explanations for everything that went down this summer—you just don't wanna hear them. It's like you need me to be the bad guy. But I got news for you, buddy. You're not so fuckin' innocent." With those words, I shut the door and stalked toward the RV.

Asshole.

He was the last person I saw before bed, the last one on my mind. And the first one I thought about when I woke up, then the first I saw too.

Newly showered, moderately hungover, and with a carrier full of two lazy fur balls, I yawned and left the RV and—fuck. I had to go back. I almost forgot Teddy's gift.

Take two.

"You're not makin' a move to change seats," I noted, opening the door to the back where I could strap in the carrier.

"Correct. It's possible you still have alcohol in your blood."

"Or you like my truck more than you like me."

He laughed through a yawn. "That too—definitely."

Nice.

I rounded the truck and got in, and I was glad I'd brought a bottle of water. Despite having guzzled half a gallon of water and two cups of coffee already, my mouth felt desert dry.

I noticed we were equally ambitious about this morning's wardrobe choices. I didn't know where his sweats and hoodie came from, but mine were all about the Bulldogs, including my ball cap.

"What the hell is in that box?" He checked the rearview as he turned the truck around. "It's huge."

"Thanks, darlin', I get that a lot. And you'll find out soon enough."

Soph always dreaded my gifts for Teddy, who did the opposite. My birthday presents and Christmas gifts were, in his eyes, epic. And he was right.

I chugged some water and got comfortable. It wasn't often I got to be the passenger.

Sebastian drove us toward Cedar Valley, and the ride was quiet. I knew we'd left things unsaid last night, but the ball was in his court. If he wanted to talk shit out, he knew where to find me. Today wasn't the day I pushed for anything.

He kept going, so I figured he was heading for the big-box stores south of town. It was where I did my shopping too. I hadn't had the time or death wish to consider checking out the malls and shopping streets.

"Oh, so this is Cedar Point." I peered out the window. This was where Dylan had picked up the RV somewhere. He'd mentioned a showroom. But in between Target, Staples, Old Navy, and a bunch of other big players, it was hard to spot the little ones. "All you need now is a Costco."

"We have one closer to the border." He made a turn and reached the parking lot of the grocery store. "Something's been bugging me since last night."

"Only since then?"

He sighed, clearly not in the mood for me. "You said I needed you to be the bad guy. Why the fuck would I do that?"

How should I know?

Lord.

"Fuck if I know. Maybe it's easier for you?" I unbuckled my belt once he'd pulled into a parking space, and I reached between the seats to open the carrier. "You're the one who was neurotic about lines not being crossed. You kept your distance and got weird if I did anything that might be considered sweet." I had a feeling the boys would stay in the carrier, but they had the travel pen to tumble around in now. "Oppy, Percy, be good, ya hear? Daddy will be back in a bit."

Oppy's ear twitched. That was the only reaction I got.

I suppressed a sigh of my own and climbed out of the truck. God knew I loved those two pups with all my heart, but I missed having a partner. Rosie had been a partner. We'd worked side by side for years.

While Sebastian stewed silently to himself, we headed into the store, and I grabbed a cart.

"Check us out, buying breakfast like an old married couple,"

I joked.

He side-eyed me with a slight twist of his lips. "You'd be more like a little brother."

"Screw you, I'm older." By a whole year.

"I didn't say younger." The fucker patted me on the head.

I elbowed his side and then aimed for the in-store bakery.

The drive to his house was silent too, to the point where I nearly jumped in my seat when he did speak up, about five minutes before we reached his house.

"Last night, you said I wasn't so innocent either," he said. "What did I do to you?"

I scratched my jaw.

I'd said that? Christ almighty, I needed to learn how to shut my trap when I was drunk. With the way things were between us, there wasn't a chance in hell I could be honest with him. The man barely tolerated me. Admitting to him he'd had that kind of power over me...fuck no. The two people I trusted the most in the world were so dang certain that my anxiousness and all those absurd reactions and emotions I'd had this summer were due to *feelings*. I'd supposedly developed feelings for Sebastian, and while I was a pro at living in denial, the evidence was pretty damning.

Moreover, it'd gotten worse. I was still so ridiculously drawn to him. His insults bit me harder. It'd hurt to see him talking to that other dude yesterday, 'cause I'd been able to feel him slipping through my fingers, and he hadn't even been mine to begin with. The power and ability to evoke that kind of jealousy and other shitty feelings remained in his grasp, and that was terrifying. I didn't want him to have that control.

Or, if I searched deep down and was honest with myself, I

did want him to possess that ability, but I wanted it to go both ways. And other dudes could fuck all the way off. So basically, I wanted my harmful drug all to myself, kinda like what we'd shared a few months ago, only without the expiration date this time.

What might one call that?

"Cat got your tongue?" he asked.

I shook my head and drummed my fingers along my knee. "Just tryin' to remember... I was drunk. I don't know."

He didn't buy it.

Tiger Lily had grown a lot since I'd last seen her. The kitten was now bigger than Oppy and Percy, and she and Echo were curious to meet the boys. Mischa oversaw the whole exchange but didn't get involved.

"It's good to see you again too, buddy." I squatted down on the living room floor and gave Mischa some attention. He stretched his neck and looked awfully pleased as I scratched him. "You're a good boy, aren't you?"

He huffed and licked my cheek.

In the meantime, Sebastian messed around in the kitchen to prepare breakfast.

"I'll give you all the cuddles later," I promised. "I'm just gonna help your daddy."

"Daddy doesn't need help," Sebastian said from the kitchen.

"Daddy might need professional help," I whispered to Mischa.

Sebastian was setting up an impressive buffet on the bar that separated the kitchen from the living room, so I assumed we'd grab our food there and then... Well, he didn't have a dining area indoors, not counting the three stools at the bar.

"We're not eating on the porch, are we?"

He furrowed his brow. "Why would we do that? We'll sit there." He nodded at the couch and chairs in front of his tiny TV.

"You never know. You Washington folk seem impervious to the cold."

"True, we're not weaklings like you Southerners."

I had to laugh at that. "So you're saying the bitching you did about the mediocre heat this summer was what, you flexin' your muscles?"

He set down a giant jar of Nutella on the bar with a bit too much force. "How about we don't talk about this summer at all anymore? It happened, it's over, let's move on."

It was a cold shower at the same time as it triggered a spark of anger, because I was fed up. "You're never gonna let this go, are you?" I was unable to mask that I was ticked off. "You don't wanna talk shit out—you just wanna stick to your assumptions and—"

"There's nothing to talk about!" he snapped. "There's no reason to either. You're leaving soon anyway, aren't you? Their house will be done before next summer's over."

"Those are your fuckin' assumptions, Sebastian!" I yelled, getting heated way too fast. "You don't know a goddamn thing, because you don't wanna have that conversation with me!"

"There's no point!" he shouted back. "You say one thing and do another—I have *no* reason to hear you out!"

Suddenly, the dogs started barking. Or Echo and Mischa. They ran for the door, and a beat later, I heard the sound of car doors closing. *Fuck.* They were here. It was Teddy's birthday.

Sebastian and I exchanged a quick, impatient look. He was probably done. I wasn't. But either way, we had to put our shit on hold and plaster grins on our faces for the birthday boy.

This wasn't over, though. Sebastian could fucking dream.

Despite all the insecurities he'd brought out in me, last night had made me bolder. He hadn't been able to resist me either. Physically, we still had something.

I was ready to play dirty.

I was the one who'd fucked up initially. So while I hoped he eventually came around to hear me out properly, it was my job to get him there. No more of this "the ball's in his court." For once in my fucking life, I wasn't gonna quit.

Teddy barged in, and it took me a beat to realize what I was looking at, my mind still stuck on Sebastian. But I knew those colors. Blue and gold. *Sweet Jesus.*

"Uncle Blake, you're already here!" he exclaimed, darting forward.

He crashed into me, and I let out a surprised laugh as I processed his Halloween costume. The kid was *me*. He was decked out in full football gear and even wore my jersey number from my high school glory days.

Soph must've ordered it straight from home. The uniform had received a couple upgrades since we were in high school. Back in the day, the top was dark blue and the pants were gold. These days, the uniform was all blue and had gold stripes along the sides.

"Happy birthday, champ," I chuckled. "You look awfully familiar."

He beamed at me and turned around, and there it was in gold letters. "Kidd 4." Same on the helmet.

"I'm you!" he replied excitedly. "And, look!" He pointed to the eye-black stickers on his cheeks. Or maybe—hot damn— maybe it was the scar Soph had painted on his cheekbone. I'd gotten my scar after an accident. Soph had been...nine or ten years old. She'd fallen off a haybale, and I'd made a run for it, managing to dive right before she hit the ground so she'd landed on top of me. In the process, I'd hit my face on a rock.

I'd been the hero of the entire ranch that year, and I'd returned to school with a cool scar.

"You look fantastic, buddy." I grinned and touched the captain's patch on his arm. "I'mma need a picture of you later."

"Momma took a thousand!" Teddy laughed and promptly announced he had to show Sebastian his costume too. The man in question was waiting in the kitchen doorway, watching with an indulgent smile.

"Look, Bastian, I'm Uncle Blake! He was a quarterback when he was little."

I zeroed in on Soph and Dylan instead, and they passed the other two in the hallway and joined me in the living room.

"Talk about attention to detail, sis." I hugged her to me and kissed the top of her head.

"I did good, huh? It took me two weeks to get the art on the helmet right." She smiled proudly.

"I'm impressed." I assumed she'd looked through all the pictures she could find from back then. "How's my li'l Bella?" My niece was strapped to Dylan's chest in some snug-as-a-bug carrier that looked more like a stretchy sheet wrapped around his torso.

"She's a daddy's girl, that's how she is," Soph grumbled. "I swear, all she does around me is scream, but the second he swoops her up, she's smiling and cooing."

"She's exaggerating," Dylan told me with a wry smirk. "Isabella does prefer it when I'm the one changing her diaper, though. But that feels more like a punishment."

I laughed.

Soph did too. "Actually, I don't mind that part."

I bet.

A minute or so later, Dylan said he was gonna heat up a bottle for the little one, so he excused himself to go to the kitchen. And it was probably for the best, because I wanted to talk football with my sister, and the Washington folk just didn't seem to appreciate that. So far, I hadn't met a single Seahawk fan in Camassia, nor had I spotted any caps or other gear with college team logos. No, wait, there'd been one. I'd seen someone wearing a Huskies scarf in town.

"You lookin' forward to the game on Saturday?" I asked.

Soph frowned immediately. "No, because I have to freaking work. It sucks. But I made reservations at that sports bar I told you about. One for the game against Auburn, and the other for Georgia Tech."

Those were the two most important games, so that was good. It was gonna be a great football month with several big games. "Are reservations really necessary?" I figured with the time zones and all, the bar should be empty that early.

"It is if we wanna get in on the dining," Soph replied. "The lunch games are decent, but the breakfast games—I swear to you, I haven't had food that awesome outside of the South. The game against Georgia Tech is early—around nine, I think—so I reserved breakfast baskets. They're to die for."

Food served in baskets was my favorite. "Nothing can go wrong when food comes in a basket."

"Right?!" She slapped my arm. "You get it. I gotta tell you, Blake, it's really good to have you back here. Someone who finally wants to catch games with me."

I chuckled but felt bad for her. Once we'd gotten older, she and I had kinda hung out in the same group of friends back home, and we'd had a solid squad for games and tailgate parties.

"By the way, I'm totally not getting involved, but did you spend the night here?" she asked curiously.

I smirked. "The man can't be in the same room with me for five minutes without hurling an insult, but he'd let me sleep in his house?"

"Ouch." She winced. "I didn't know it was still that bad. I thought y'all were making progress."

I wasn't sure screwing in the parking lot was considered progress. If anything, it felt like the opposite, because Sebastian grew angrier, and I'd lost my resolve to stay away from the man. All the warnings, the red flags, the promises I'd made to myself—fucking gone.

"It's difficult to make progress when he refuses to listen to me," I said.

Soph quirked a brow at me. "Since when did that stop you? Make him listen. You gotta understand that, in his eyes, you had no excuse or explanation. You up and left just because it was easy. He sees the deceit—you spent so much time with him and didn't mention a word about the program for Teddy in Georgia, and you know how Sebastian feels about Teddy. They're so close, Blake." She paused and offered a fond little grin. "In a way, they became best friends before Sebastian and I did."

I furrowed my brow. "Didn't you know Sebastian before Teddy was born?"

She shrugged. "We were friends—but, first and foremost, neighbors. It wasn't until a while after Axel split that Sebastian and I grew closer. He's not that easy to get to know, to be honest. But if there's one thing Sebastian can't handle, it's people abandoning others, so he must've lowered his guard for me when Teddy and I stood there without Axel one day."

I remembered that. David had flown out for a week. Teddy had been two or three. I hadn't been able to get off work, but she'd brought Teddy to see me shortly after David returned home. I'd been living in Savannah at the time, which I suspected was the only reason she'd agreed to stay with me for a few weeks. Things had been ice-cold between her and our folks at the time.

"Sebastian told me about his parents flakin' out on him and his sister a lot growing up," I mentioned quietly.

Soph nodded. "He's a man with countless acquaintances and very few friends because of that."

Sebastian had told me that too.

And then I had bailed on him.

"I have hope for you two, though," Soph murmured. "You got under his skin in a way I haven't seen anyone else do. But you gotta do damage control. He genuinely believes you tried to take Teddy—and me—away from him. Or them. Or Washington —you know what I mean. Because of the program. He doesn't know you bought that land for us before you learned Teddy's aid got cut. So I don't care if he won't listen to you. Shove the deed in his face and make him see the date or something. Show him that you had no intention of being a sneak and shipping us off to Georgia."

That wasn't bad advice. Hell, I had all the info on my phone. I could show him right now.

"When you say you have hope for us..." I trailed off.

She patted my arm. "This is where you grow up and admit you actually want something serious with Sebastian."

I waited for the panic to tie a noose around my neck—any minute now. It was coming. Me? Getting serious with someone? With *Sebastian*...? Heh. I cleared my throat and shifted where I stood. A trickle of nerves definitely dropped to my stomach, but as I glanced into the kitchen and spotted Sebastian helping Teddy open the big jar of Nutella, I wasn't sure I could count those nerves as a warning to find the nearest exit.

I wasn't stupid. I'd skirted around the term for weeks, especially when thinking back on what he and I had shared. But now, my sister was forcing me to put it at the forefront of my mind. Something serious meant *relationship*.

"You can't even look away from him," Soph accused with glee in her eyes.

I threw her an annoyed look, because she had to hold her damn horses here. It was way too soon to discuss any type of future with Sebastian. For one, I didn't think he'd ever be interested. For two, hope was a dangerous thing, and I'd never been in a real relationship before. I'd fuck that up in a day.

I shook my head, getting anxious at the mere thought. Once upon a time, I'd walked away from a football career because I couldn't handle the pressure. I'd had people coming to watch me from across the East Coast. But no scholarship mattered when I spent two hours before every game on the shitter. If nothing came out on the lower end, there was always the upper. My senior year of high school, I could've been the poster child for Pepto.

On the other hand, Sebastian wasn't a football game. I remembered nights and early mornings when we sought each other out in bed, half awake, half asleep, 100% constantly drawn to the other. And the feeling—that very feeling—when he snuck my leg between his and hitched his leg over my hip, or the other way around, and our arms fused us together, I'd been fucking blissful. Jesus Christ, I'd been so at ease. It'd felt so right.

I took a deep breath and felt how those memories released the tightness around my chest.

Maybe I wasn't ready to think or hope for a relationship, but I knew one thing. I wanted more nights with him. I *missed* him —like fucking crazy. I missed his stupidly charming grins and how, with a single look, he could make me wanna drop to my knees.

"Momma!" Teddy yelled. "Dad and Sebastian say, stop whispering secrets—we're gonna eat breakfast now!"

The birthday boy had spoken.

After breakfast, I was ready for Teddy to open gifts.

So was he.

Sebastian said the boy had ants in his pants, and that was an apt description.

"Let's get ours out of the way before Blake outshines us all," Soph joked.

"We all have our superpowers," I said. This was mine. I already knew what I was giving Teddy for Christmas. A drum kit.

In a couple minutes, plates and coffee mugs were replaced by presents on the coffee table in the living room, and I was admittedly curious about Sebastian's gifts to him. I counted four of them.

Dylan and I occupied the chairs on the ends of the table, while Sebastian and Soph had Teddy between them on the couch, so they handed him the gifts. First one was from Soph.

"First up is a gift from Mama," I said in my best sports commentator voice. "Let's hope it's not another 2017 fiasco."

Dylan barked out a laugh at that one, which he immediately tried to silence upon noticing Soph's glare.

"Momma, I love your gifts also!" Teddy was quick to say, and he enveloped Soph in a hug, football gear still on, before opening the gift. Though, the helmet had come off around the same time Dylan had put Isabella down for a nap upstairs. "Is it underwear?" Teddy shook the soft package.

I felt my shoulders shake with laughter. Such a typical mama gift.

It was, in fact, underwear. Soph defended herself, saying there were a few "necessities" before the fun started.

Two T-shirts, underwear, socks—for fucking real, sis—and a beanie and scarf. Then she upped the game a little with a pillowcase, an action figure, and a lunch box from Teddy's favorite superhero franchise. He was all about the Flash, that one.

They were good gifts, no doubt, and Teddy was stoked. But Dylan hadn't been swayed thus far; he still preferred to buy his own gift for Teddy.

"We welcome Daddy onto the field," I narrated. "He knows it's going to be hard to top last year's gift when Teddy got his very own iPod." Which, in reality, was Dylan's old iPhone. But Teddy couldn't really handle a phone yet, so they'd hidden the phone icon in the lower menu bar. He could send texts, listen to music, and play a couple games on it. He loved the thing.

"Funny you should mention that," Dylan mused.

Teddy tore up the wrapping and ended up with two gifts in one. "Oh wow!" He recognized the phone case first.

"It's waterproof, buddy," Dylan told him. "Now you can listen to music in the bathtub."

Teddy's eyes lit up like a Christmas tree. "I can have it in the water?"

"Yup. Neat, huh?"

"Neat!" Teddy echoed, nodding. The second gift was just as cool, a Bluetooth speaker, and Daddy had done it again. Full score. The imaginary crowd went wild.

"Daddy faces stiff competition from Sebastian Wilder, though," I commentated. "I don't need to remind y'all how he saved the day last year when Uncle Blake's gift arrived late."

Teddy giggled. "You're so funny, Uncle Blake."

Even Sebastian threw me a mildly amused glance.

The imaginary crowd went wild at that too.

Oof, Sebastian definitely earned his fifteen minutes of fame. He gave Teddy a pair of ice skates, a couple books, and a customized hockey helmet.

"It's the Flash!" Teddy was over the moon. He inspected the

red helmet and pointed to all the little details in the artwork. "It looks like he's holding my name!"

"That's so amazing, Teddy," Soph murmured. "How on earth...? It looks painted on. I was cutting little vinyl pieces until my eyes were bleeding when I did his football helmet."

Sebastian cleared his throat. "One of the kids at the Quad is a fantastic artist. I gave him free rein and a weekend job." He'd given the kid more than that. It was what Sebastian did, I'd come to learn. He made those children believe in themselves.

Teddy put on his new helmet with a satisfied grin and declared he was ready for the last gift.

I obeyed and pushed the big box closer to him, and he stood up to be able to remove the bow from the top.

"Should we get the fire extinguisher ready?" Soph teased.

I merely grinned and scratched my nose.

She knew what the lack of an answer meant. "Oh God."

"Teddy, do you remember Troy from Georgia?" I asked.

Teddy immediately looked my way, and his mouth popped open.

"I'm getting the fire extinguisher," Soph said abruptly and rose from her seat.

I laughed.

"Who's Troy?" Sebastian's forehead creased with confusion.

"He's so awesome!" Teddy literally shouted, waking up the dogs in the process.

"I've only heard rumors," Dylan chuckled.

"He's a buddy of mine from back home," I replied. "Soph was best friends with his little sister in high school, and we try to get together whenever she brings Teddy to visit our folks."

"He's a bad influence!" Soph hollered from the hallway.

I shook my head in amusement. "Troy runs a business specializin' in special effects for movies and entertainment."

"He makes explosions and fires and wave machines and,

and, and I ran through blue smoke on his ranch, Bastian," Teddy rambled excitedly. "Blue smoke!" Then he returned to opening the gift, a bit more vigorously now, eager to see what was inside.

"Okay, I'm ready." Soph huffed and came back with the fire extinguisher. She wasn't joking around.

On the other hand, neither was Troy.

"Is this gift legal?" Soph asked.

I shrugged. "Why wouldn't it be?"

She sighed impatiently. "Let me rephrase. Is it legal to use the way it's intended?"

"Oh, probably not." I wasn't worried, though. Particularly not considering our location. The beach would be perfect to try it out. "You're thinkin' about the miniature fireball air balloons he and I made before college, aren't you?"

The cops hadn't been too pleased to spot several tiny air balloons over the fields that one evening. Less so when they all exploded and set off fireworks in the air. But did anyone get hurt? Nope. Not a single glowing ember landed in the field. Troy knew what he was doing.

"Yeah, no fucking shit." Soph had lost her filters.

"Oh, Momma, look!" Teddy lifted his new toy from the box, a quite heavy RC car Troy had built himself. It was about a foot in length, and I'd ordered two of them. Both were designed to look like monster trucks. One black and one metallic blue.

"They're ready to run, champ," I told him.

Teddy was the best fucking kid to buy gifts for. He got so dang excited, and he showed it.

"Before we show everyone else, we need to have a secret talk," I said. "I'll tell you everythin' you need to know about the features."

He nodded, eyes wide and full of anticipation.

CHAPTER
7

Fifteen minutes later, Teddy and I walked down the private pathway from Sebastian's house to the beach. We had AC/DC blasting from the Bluetooth speaker Teddy had clipped on to his pants, and we each carried an RC car that was going to blow some minds.

This was our action scene. We had our mean game faces on, and the others were waiting for us in the sand, Sebastian with Mischa and Echo, Soph with the fire extinguisher.

"Thunderstruck" reached its climax as I instructed Dylan to film the magic. Then we set down the cars and completed a test drive to put some distance between us and the new gadgets.

Teddy struggled to withhold his grin. He'd asked me if we could look "badass," and I couldn't deny him. Of course we were gonna do this lookin' badass as fuck.

The waves rolled in and washed up along the empty beach, sending salty spray and the smell of kelp into the cold air.

"Be careful," Soph pleaded. "Blake, you know who you're dealin' with here."

"I'm well aware, Mama," I drawled. I turned my ball cap on backward as "Highway to Hell" started, and it was the perfect song. "Just step aside and let us men handle this."

Sebastian snorted.

"Yeah, we got this, Momma," Teddy said coolly.

With our devices in hand, we maneuvered our monster trucks around to face us, both waiting some 150 feet up the beach.

Teddy and I exchanged a firm nod before we started. I directed my blue truck down to the bank where the waves rolled in, driving it through the foamy wash, and Teddy followed with the black truck. Then up again, over and around the sandy terrain.

In my periphery, I noticed Echo following the movements closely. Hell, it would be fun watching him chase the trucks.

"You ready, champ?"

"Super ready." Teddy jogged in place, unable to stand still. "Now?"

"Now." We flipped the orange switches on the devices, and then I had to get Teddy's reaction. I watched his whole face light up as the trucks were engulfed in flames, sending big fireballs up into the air.

To Troy's credit, it really did look like the trucks exploded. But that wasn't enough for my buddy.

"Gah!" Teddy gasped, pointed, and stared wide-eyed. Because these trucks didn't merely explode. They survived. They emerged from the fire and kept going. "Uncle Blake!"

Fuck, my mask slipped off completely. Almost forty years old, and this shit still got me going. "I *know*. How fuckin' cool is that? Troy built them to be able to take on fire and all kinds of shit. You can blow them up over and over." We just had to refill the little fuel tank and replace a part for the ignition. "I reckon there's enough gas for one more explosion. You wanna go?"

"Uh, *yeah*! Dad, film it again, please!"

"I'm filming the whole thing, buddy," Dylan promised, chuckling.

Wanting to see how far I could push the truck I was driving,

I fell to my knees and sat back on the heels of my shoes, and I got into it. Everything around me ceased to exist, except for Teddy and the black truck. This was just for us.

"Come Fourth of July, I bet we can make the trucks explode confetti," I said.

"That would be awesome!" Teddy maneuvered his truck expertly. People automatically underestimated him most of the time, and it bugged me. He loved gadgets. He was smarter than many gave him credit for. It was as if people judged a person's intelligence by their motor skills. It was fucked up.

"Check this out." I eased my thumb onto the top of the little joystick and guided the truck up a sandbank with a smoother turn. Then I sped up right before the edge and flew off it. A ball of fire erupted from the tank. "Yeehaw, motherfucker." ...And I completely failed to do a flip. Fuck. Next time. I grinned.

"Yeehaw!" Teddy echoed. "Can we do this all day?"

I let out a laugh. "It might get too cold for that. But I'll tell you what—next time you have a sleepover at my place, we'll see what fun we can come up with. Sometimes, you just wanna watch shit blow up. Am I right?"

"You are right," he laughed. "Blow shit up, blow shit up!"

And the crowd went wild.

I'm not tired, I'm not tired, I'm not tired.

After an intense birthday celebration that morning, everyone had gone their separate ways. Soph, Dylan, Teddy, and Bella were heading over to Dylan's parents', and I crashed with my boys as soon as I got into the RV. They snuggled up beside me, and we slept for hours.

It should've been enough. I'd showered, put on my nice jeans, a button-down, and my best cologne, and I'd talked myself into a good mood for an evening in a bowling alley. Then I'd met up with everyone again, and I'd greeted the evident disco theme with a yawn.

Now I couldn't stop.

I blamed the darkness in here. The lanes were lit up with UV lights, and the place was packed with Halloween decorations. Hell, there was even a giant disco ball in the ceiling, casting moving flickers all over. And the music... Pop music blared from the speakers. Kids were hopped up on sugar from trick-or-treating, and parents were nursing their exhaustion with beer.

I finished last in our first game. Soph finished first, followed by Sebastian.

Dylan and Teddy were looking forward to their revenge.

I was looking forward to going home to get more sleep.

While the others took a break to finish their orders of wings and grilled cheese, I volunteered to get us more drinks and snacks. I needed to be on my feet. If I spent another minute sitting down, I'd fall asleep. Despite the hideous disco music.

The bar was actually calmer than the lanes. Considering what day it was, the place wasn't crowded; the kids who were here just happened to be fucking loud. Combined with the music and the incessant sound of pins hitting the floor, I was just waiting for the headache to set in.

"Hey...can I get, uh—" I squinted at the menu behind the bar. "One order of fried pickles, one buffalo wings, and two orders of fries, please. Oh, and two beers and three Cokes."

"We can bring the snacks to your lane," the bartender offered.

"Much appreciated, but I don't mind waitin'." In fact, I insisted.

I slid onto the nearest stool and nodded in thanks as he set two beers on a tray.

As I took a sip of my beer, I nearly jumped in my seat when Sebastian appeared next to me.

"Soph wants a churro too," he said.

Because who didn't go to a bowling alley in northern Washington for the best churros?

"Dip a French fry in sugar," I replied. "She won't know the difference."

He let out a laugh, and he couldn't fucking know how fantastic that sounded. It was pathetic, but the next breath came easier.

Something had happened over the day. He'd gone from being mostly quiet during our morning festivities to taking the wheel tonight. He and Soph had enjoyed the game.

Once Sebastian had gotten his churro order in, he settled onto the stool next to mine and stole my beer to take a swig.

This was new.

Shouldn't he run back to the others now?

"I have a bone to pick with you," he said.

This was less new.

"You have more than one, darlin'."

He tipped his head in a silent *touché*. "Either way, I—" He threw an irritated glance at the ceiling, then leaned closer to me. "Follow me. I can't hear my own thoughts in here."

Bullshit. It wasn't that loud in the bar.

Was he gonna murder me now? He knew a lot of hiding spots in the woods.

I took another gulp of beer and watched him walk away. Toward the bathrooms. Fuck. Yeah, I followed. How could I not? What were we gonna fight about this time? And would it lead to sex? Only the last question was important.

He led the way to a narrow hallway and ducked into what turned out to be an empty coat-check room.

"Please tell me you brought lube instead of a rubber this time," I half joked.

He flicked on the light and left the door open. Bummer.

"You're a real comedian, Blake," he deadpanned. "We're not screwing again."

"All right." I admit, I was disappointed. It seemed like the perfect location for a repeat of last time.

He folded his arms over his chest and turned into someone most people didn't wanna meet in a dark alley.

That side of him didn't intimidate me. Outside of the bedroom, no one had any power over me.

"Then what do you want?" I frowned and folded up the sleeves of my shirt. Casual was always the best way to provoke when facing hostility.

"It's easier to kick a bad habit when you don't have to worry about it," he stated. I was the bad habit? Of course I was. "I've been watching you all day—you can't make up another lie about how little you eat these days. You barely touched your breakfast, you didn't eat during the game—" he nodded in the direction of the lanes "—and I bet you didn't eat at home either."

"Did too," I blurted out defensively. Truth be told, I was confused. I was a grown-ass man; I hadn't had anyone watching my food intake in decades. I didn't know how to feel about it. "I had a donut."

He offered me a bitchy look at that. "Quit trying to give me more grief, Blake."

"Goddammit—I'm not!" I threw out my arms, both exasperated and bewildered. Why did he fucking care? "First of all, I'm flattered you watched me all day. Second, I don't want you to kick me like a bad habit. Third, I haven't lost any damn weight. I eat just fine."

He didn't believe me, and he was evidently going to prove it, because he closed the distance between us. And before I had the chance to hope, hell, maybe I'd get laid after all, he lifted my shirt and tugged at my belt. Just to reveal that I wasn't using the regular hole in the leather.

He made my head swim. Maybe I was too tired to focus on the topic he wanted to push for some unknown reason. I didn't care. Perhaps I'd lost a few pounds; I wasn't one to keep track. When work was busy—fuck, I wasn't even gonna humor him. Sometimes life got in the way. Big fucking whoop. I felt all right. More than all right—because of the close proximity. He was my bad habit too. As soon as I got a whiff of him, my mouth watered and I wanted to crawl back under his skin.

I flicked my gaze to his face and waited for him to lift his stare too.

Look at us, darlin'. We're a mess for each other.

He had to see it, didn't he?

I had to give him something. Right now.

"I never tried to get Soph and Teddy to move to Georgia," I said. "I joked about it—I missed having her close. I was jealous because I was missin' out on Teddy's childhood. But I swear to you, I never actively tried to get them to move home." The urgency to spill it all rushed through me, causing me to almost stumble over my words. I just didn't want him to stop me or seek the nearest exit. "Over the years, I managed to save up some money, so I bought the land. I get by—I only have myself. But they've been strugglin', and it was one good deed I couldn't fuck up. I bought it the first week I was in town this summer."

He wouldn't look up from my belt, but I knew I had his attention. I also sensed the tension rolling off him. Not in the way that he was relaxing from listening to me—no, he was getting more and more tense. But I had to keep talking. I had to make him understand.

"When I heard about Teddy's aid gettin' cut, I mentioned it to our mother," I went on. "She found the program, and I pushed for it. I did. Because I didn't think they had any other choice—and it woulda been temporary. It wasn't some ugly move to get them to leave their home permanently, Sebastian."

"That's enough." His voice came out gravelly, and the low and rich timbre shook me. Fucking hell, how I wanted him. "I don't wanna hear another word."

"No, we have to—"

He shook his head and looked up at long last, and the conflict burning in his eyes seared into my skull. He was fucking desperate to put distance between us, and he was failing. He cupped my jaw and kissed me before I could say something. Which was...dangerously effective. He short-circuited my brain the second he swept his tongue into my mouth.

Finally.

Every kiss was a reunion.

Finally.

A nail in the coffin. My coffin. Soon, I'd be completely lost in my surrender.

His hands dropped to my hips as mine slid along his arms, up to his jaw, and eventually to the back of his neck. The kiss grew heated, and he pressed me against the wall.

Finally.

He broke away to catch his breath and rested our foreheads together. "You have to let me forget you."

Screw that.

I clenched my jaw and shook my head. "Fuck you, Wilder. That ain't happenin'."

He wasn't merely looking to change the course of what we had been, what we were, and what we could be. He was trying to reach a point where he could say goodbye and...

Christ. He really had no clue. He didn't know I was planning on sticking around. Would he even believe me if I said I was probably moving here?

I kissed him hard and reached for his belt. "I'm not goin' anywhere." I spoke against his lips as I dipped a hand into his jeans. My commando beast. "I'm done runnin'." With those words, I sank to my knees and pulled his cock free.

He shook his head and scrubbed his hands over his face, but he didn't have the strength to say anything. Instead, he caved. His fingers disappeared in my hair, and he grabbed a tight fistful before he guided his long, thick cock into my mouth.

It'd been too damn long for me to try to pretend as if I wasn't dying to worship his cock. A moan escaped me, and I closed my eyes to shut everything else out. I traced the length of him with my tongue, I sucked at the head, and I grazed my teeth along the ridges.

He better not make me beg to get my throat fucked.

I gave him everything. I sucked him long and hard, over and over drawing him down to where I choked around him. It seemed to get him going, thank fuck. His breathing became labored, and he couldn't remain still anymore.

"You make me weak."

Good. I opened my eyes again and peered up at him. I wanted him weak for me.

He landed a hand on the wall behind me and started thrusting deeper, forcing himself down my throat. And he lingered. He got off on watching me choose his cock over oxygen. Each breathless second was a moment where he was the god of my world. Each push drove me closer to a light-headed state of bliss and subservience. Here, he owned me. Here, the power belonged solely to him.

"Jesus fuck, baby." He touched my cheek. "Those eyes—I see what a complete cock whore you are for me."

Finally.

A shudder ripped down my spine. My cock strained against the zipper in my jeans. His filthy affection washed over me, and

I redoubled my efforts. I tightened my lips around him and sucked him harder, wetter, deeper. I swallowed around him repeatedly and died the best death whenever he groaned at the feel of my convulsing throat muscles squeezing his cock.

He began chasing his orgasm. My lungs burned, my eyes stung, and none of it mattered because he got me there. The oxygen deprivation sent me flying into a sacred space I hadn't experienced until this man. But he didn't let me soar very far. He inched out of my mouth and rubbed the wet head of his cock against my lips, smearing them with pre-come and saliva.

"Breathe, boy." His low command did nothing to stave off my own need to come. "Open wide. I have something for you."

"*Hnghh.*" I swallowed and opened my mouth, feeling drowsy and approximately two seconds away from getting off. I just needed *something.*

"That's it," he groaned, breathing heavily. He stroked his big, beautiful, glistening cock right in front of my face, and I wanted to suck it again. Fuck, I craved it. I licked my lips, and he chuckled, completely out of breath. "Now. Drink me. Swallow me."

I couldn't help it. The moment the first burst of come landed on my tongue, I cupped my cock through my jeans and squeezed and rubbed—anything to alleviate the pressure. At the same time, I drank him down until he was almost done. That was when he let me suck him off again, and I buried him in my throat and swallowed every drop.

"Holy—" He exhaled a long groan and shivered violently.

The next time he withdrew from me, he did it slowly and gave me the chance to lick and suck him clean.

"Good boy," he panted. "Get up here."

I was off my knees before he got the last word out, and he spun us around so he was leaning back against the wall.

"Show me how desperate you are." The fucker angled me so

my cock pressed against his thigh. "Rub yourself right here, and if you do a good job, I'll finger-fuck you until you come in your jeans."

Jesus. I didn't know how he could make me feel so pathetic and turned on at the same time. And I was too horny to find answers. I swallowed and tried to kill the nerves that spiked.

"No—don't lower your eyes. Come here." He coaxed me closer and dipped down to kiss me. That was better. "I love tasting myself on you," he whispered. Fuck, yeah. "Obey me, Blake. Let me watch you debase yourself."

A weird, pleading sound slipped from between my lips, and his words reverberated through me, packing a punch I hadn't felt before. The good kind of punch.

"You're so fuckin' dirty," I mumbled.

He smiled into a deep, hungry kiss that melted away my shame.

I...I'd do anything for him.

I kissed him back and locked my arms around his neck, and then I...pushed my cock against his thigh. And the slightest pressure ignited me.

"Keep going." He undid my belt. Then I felt one of his hands glide down my ass. "This is what you get. Fuck—your ass. I've missed it. I miss tongue-fucking you until you lose your voice."

Heat rushed to the surface, and I threw myself into the kiss, into the moment, because fuck it. Sebastian had shown me what sex was all about. Everything he'd done to me had taken me to new heights.

"I miss your bed," I admitted. "Your shower. The, uh..." God, that felt way too good to be acceptable at my age. "The balcony upstairs."

He hummed and seduced me with his tongue, teasing it around mine.

He squeezed my ass every time I rubbed against his thigh, and I'd stopped caring. It felt fucking amazing. Filthy. A little humiliating. And so fucking needy.

"There we go. There's the greedy man who'll take anything I give to get off." He finally gave me more. He slipped a hand down my boxer briefs and pressed two fingers against my asshole. "You want this?"

I nodded quickly and rolled my hips over his thigh. "Please."

Sweet mother of—I really was a cock whore for him. Not to mention an ass whore. Whenever he stuck something inside me, I was in heaven. I rode his fingers and thrust against his thigh over and over, until I couldn't regulate my breathing anymore and had to break away from his lips. I buried my face against his neck instead and sucked on his flesh.

"Have you let anyone else play with your tight little ass since we fucked around, Blake?"

"God—" I moaned and clenched around him, needing that sting. "No. Fuck no." Perhaps those were the magic words to something, because we reached a new level of carnal desire, and we met in another kiss that sealed the deal for me. I was ready for the final nail in the coffin and everything that entailed, as long as I could get a hit whenever I wanted for the rest of my life.

"I'm not a mistake." I screwed my eyes shut and sucked in a breath as the orgasm unfurled within me.

With a third finger forced into my ass, he pushed me over the edge and set my climax on fire. Or maybe it was the layer of mortification that made me feel like I was burning.

The pleasure overtook me, overwhelmed me, and was prolonged by his dirty whispers. He wanted to film me fucking myself on a vibrator mounted in the shower. He wanted to watch me stroke myself off in front of him. He wanted to tie me to his bed and spend a day eating my ass.

I couldn't breathe. I couldn't fucking move. Every muscle in my body protested. My cock strained painfully as I coated the inside of my underwear with come, and it fucked with my head. How could I wanna roll around in that humiliating heat? Because I did. I wanted to see how far he could push me.

The waves ebbed eventually, and I managed to haul in a ragged breath.

"What a fucking mess you made of yourself." Sebastian dropped a kiss to my jaw and righted my jeans.

Taking a step back, I surveyed the damage and adjusted my cock. It made me grimace. "This is where you invite me to your place so we can continue screwin' each other's brains out, preferably after a shower."

Or during.

He let out a chuckle and shook his head. "This is the problem, Blake. When I'm near you, I can't think straight. You cloud my judgment." He scrubbed his hands over his face, and when he dropped them again, he almost appeared older. More tired. "You're not a mistake—but what we keep doing... Christ. It's not good for us."

"Are you fuckin' kiddin' me, Sebastian?" I blurted out. "Is this how it's gonna be every time? We fuck and remember how wild we are together, and then you freak out and run away? I thought that was my job." I jabbed a finger to his chest. "It pissed you off to no end when I took the coward's way out, but you're no better yourself."

That crossed a line. He raised a brow in warning. "Easy, Blake. I didn't say I was running away. I was a fool for thinking I could avoid talking to you about what happened, but you didn't let me finish." He put some distance between us by taking a couple steps away. "Go home and walk your boys." He retrieved his keys and took out the one for his Harley or ATV. Probably his bike because he'd driven it here. "Then head to my place.

Wait for me. We'll talk—but no spending the night," he added pointedly. "We're just gonna talk shit out."

Oh, for fuck's sake. Fine. I withheld an eye roll and snatched the keys from him. "Talk. Sure. We'll talk. I'll go say goodbye to the others."

Since Sebastian was gonna be a stubborn dick about things, he could have fun facing the firing squad, 'cause I was gonna duck out with a quick excuse of not feeling well.

It wasn't entirely inaccurate at this point.

CHAPTER
8

I did more than walk Oppy and Percy. I walked them, fed them, and brought them—and my laundry—with me to Sebastian's place, where I also took the liberty of showering in a bathroom that didn't require me to refill the water tank and hunch down to fit into the stall.

I rejoined the boys downstairs and tightened the draw-strings to my sweats. No underwear, no tee. Sebastian wasn't going to walk through that door and see me and think we'd talk for twenty minutes before kicking me out. In fact, there would be no sudden exits whatsoever. If we argued, we'd have to figure it out. If he wanted me to leave, he'd have to give me the chance to wait for my laundry to dry.

Percy tumbled into my ankle as I walked toward the couch, so I picked him up and got him settled between my hand and my neck. He had these periods when he was incredibly affec-tionate, and given that I was starved for cuddles, I enjoyed those moments the most.

"At least you love me, buddy." I pressed a kiss to his back and zeroed in on the pictures above Sebastian's couch.

A wall reserved for family, without question. If I knew my sister, she was the one in charge of this hall of fame, but I knew

Sebastian too. Family was important to him, and he wanted reminders of them nearby.

I hadn't taken the time to look closer last visit. It was the first time I saw Sebastian's sister and two nephews. The boys appeared to be around eight or nine in the photo, and both were trying to wrestle Sebastian to the ground. In another picture, it was Sebastian, his sister, and their...I assumed it was their grandfather. A bunch of apple trees in the background.

Teddy was otherwise the star, understandably. There was one I really liked. Teddy was maybe four or five, and he was sprawled out across Sebastian's lap in the back of Soph's car. They were both asleep.

Seeing all these pictures put a rock in the pit of my stomach, and it felt akin to grief for missing out. Missing out on ending up on walls and being part of something.

I wanted my feet to grow roots for the first time in my life.

"I'm givin' you and your brother a bath tomorrow. I can get mud out of your fur, but I can't do squat about beach sand." I smacked another kiss to Percy's back before setting him down on the soft rug.

Tiger Lily watched from the windowsill, her tail flicking gracefully. Her head tilted just a fraction of a second before Mischa and Echo darted for the front door, signaling Sebastian's homecoming.

The nerves made a swift return, but I wasn't backing out this time.

All cards on the table.

I was ready to be honest, to tell it all, and to use words I'd spent my life avoiding.

"The R-word," I muttered under my breath. "Relationship. Relationship, relationship, relationship."

I could do it.

What I wasn't sure I could handle was Sebastian's rejection.

Because I wasn't stupid. I wasn't the only one struggling with commitment. If anything, he was worse. Possibly. He *could* be worse. After all, it'd taken my sister years to become really close to him, and that was just friendship.

The door opened, and it was followed by Sebastian greeting his boys.

I got settled on the couch, ready to chain myself to any nearby object so he couldn't kick me out.

Oppy, the little traitor, jumped out to greet Sebastian too.

"Why am I not surprised to see you, little one?" he murmured. "Is your dumbass daddy doing laundry?"

I winced and scratched my ear. "I showered here too." Might as well throw that out there. "And if you call me dumbass one more time, I'll plant my sweet ass in your bed."

Sebastian sighed heavily. His keys landed somewhere, by the sound of it. Then he emerged from the hallway and looked me up and down. "Make yourself at home, I guess."

"Thanks, darlin'." I smiled. "How did the last game go?"

He went into the kitchen and opened the fridge. "We let Teddy win, and Dylan mopped the floor with me. Sophia was more interested in eating. I almost asked if she's pregnant again, but that's a mistake I won't make twice."

I grinned. "Good call."

"Mm." He grabbed a couple containers from the fridge and placed them on the bar. "If you tell me you're not hungry, we're gonna have a problem."

No, I could eat. I patted my stomach. "Feed me, Daddy. Anythin' I can do to help?"

"No," he answered right away with a side-eyed look at my abs. "You and your come gutters can stay right where you are."

I spluttered a laugh. *Come gutters.* Christ, that was a new one for me.

"You give me whiplash sometimes, Sebastian," I chuckled.

"Your insults fuckin' hurt, and your thinly veiled compliments make me feel ten feet tall." I shook my head to myself, baffled and amazed at the impact he had on me.

He furrowed his brow and busied himself with reheating food, so I reckoned he wasn't gonna respond.

It was time to get serious. I cleared my throat and shifted in my seat, pulling one knee up to the couch. "Have you thought about what I said before?"

He knew what I was referring to. The deed to the house—that I'd bought it before Teddy's aid was cut. More importantly, that I wasn't trying to get Soph and Teddy to move.

He nodded slowly, maybe unsure of how to phrase himself. I didn't know.

"I believe you," he replied quietly. "I never thought you were evil, Blake. But it takes a certain level of asshole to lie the way you did. The deceit bothered me a whole lot more than anything else. You knew about the program in Georgia for *several days*—while you spent *every* single night with me, and you didn't say a goddamn word." He stopped what he was doing and clenched his jaw. His eyes fell closed next, and he took a deep breath. "That's all I see. I remember what we did—shooting the shit, our banter, when you came over here and cooked... And now, all I can think about is what must've gone through your head. Behind every fucking smile you gave me—the lying ruined it."

"You wanna know what went through my head?" I got off the couch instantly, and I joined him on my side of the bar. "I was a mess." He had to believe me. I knew exactly what he was talking about. I'd been mulling this over for weeks too. Just like he had. "I was reeling. I got sucked in by everything we did—everything you did to me. I was so hooked, and it blindsided me. It was gonna be a few easy weeks where I didn't have to pretend to be someone else. A vacation. And..." Fuck, how did I even say this right? "What you gave me was both heaven and hell. For the first time in...shit, ever, I could be myself. I don't throw around the word love willy-nilly—hell, the opposite—but I fell head over fucking heels in love with the world *you* showed me." I paused and took a breath, realizing that my heart was pounding and my hands were sweaty. "All these reactions started comin' at me. They *hurt*—like, physically. I got anxious and worried and scared shitless. Because everything was coming to an end."

I dragged a hand over my face, frustrated that I wasn't able to convey myself properly. It didn't feel right.

"You know sometimes how you can feel somethin's wrong, but you can't pinpoint what it is?" I swallowed dryly. "That's what happened. I knew you were the cause of all these bizarre emotions in me. It could be the smallest thing, insignificant gestures—like when you made up the sofa on the balcony and we had pizza. In the grand scheme of things, that's probably not the most romantic thing someone's ever done, but I lost my footing. And after that, I had to lie to myself. I had to insist that shit was still cool—casual, no strings or whatever. And I kept coming back for more, despite that I had this voice in the back of my head yelling at me to run the other way because I was in dangerous territory, completely unfamiliar to anything I'd experienced before."

Should I keep rambling?

He wasn't making eye contact. He still had them closed, and the tension in his shoulders reached new levels.

"I am deeply sorry for goin' behind your back, Sebastian," I told him earnestly. "I should've been honest from the beginnin'. I just couldn't. Even though you were givin' me the mother of emotional roller-coaster rides and I couldn't see what those feelings meant at the time, I clung to every second I got to be with you. Time was running out, so I..." I trailed off, suddenly exhausted and wary. "I was so conflicted. Every day—torn between hightailin' it outta here so I could put myself back together, and... I'm sorry. Sometimes I wonder if it stings when you call me crap like that because you might be right. Maybe I am a dumbass. Maybe I'm a piece of shit. I'm not good at analyzing feelings, and I've never had to. With you, I didn't have a choice. It hit me outta nowhere. All of a sudden, it wasn't easy to sneak out in the middle of the night. I couldn't cut all ties and move on. You fucked me up."

I sank down onto the stool next to me and scrubbed a hand over my jaw.

"I know I was a coward," I said quietly. "I left without a word. I didn't say anythin' to you about the program. I get it. But I didn't leave because it just happened to be easier. I was in full panic mode." I cleared my throat and thought back on how I'd left. The memories were hazy at best. I barely remembered the flight, only that my mother picked me up in Atlanta. They'd stopped serving me alcohol at some point during the flight too. "I'm sorry. I didn't mean to hijack the conversation right when you got started." I might as well squeeze in one last apology before he had the floor again. If he had anything else to say. "I'm also sorry for saying you fucked me up. In a way, you did. But I'm the one who's been hiding who I am for twenty-five years. I sheltered myself from ever havin' to deal with these scenarios, and it's made me a little..." *dumb as a box of rocks.* I made a gesture at the side of my head. "Case in point, I was mad at you for weeks. Mad at myself for craving the next hit, mad at you for turning me into a junkie and an anxious mess. I called you toxic to Soph and David when I told them. I explained my reactions, and I said our fling or whatever had been toxic. They laughed in my face, of course." Seriously, what was it with this man? My nerves were shot now too. No wonder I forgot to eat sometimes. "Anyway. I know my feelings better today. I'll shut up now."

As much as I wanted to get a sense of his reaction to my word vomit, it was my turn to avoid eye contact. I didn't have the guts to face him.

It was too quiet.

I hadn't even noticed the air changing, but I felt it now, charged and heavy—and not in the good, sexy way.

Pins and fucking needles.

Eventually, with one slight movement after another, he continued preparing our food. Two generous servings of lasagna went into the microwave one by one, and in the meantime, he cut up some lettuce and green onions.

I caught him gearing up to say something a few times. He stopped what he was doing and took a breath, but instead of words coming out, he deflated with a sigh. Then he shook his head and returned to his task.

In the end, he set two plates of food on the bar and told me to bring them to the couch.

The lasagna smelled fantastic, but I wasn't sure how much I could eat when my stomach was a knotted clusterfuck of nerves and doubts. Nevertheless, I brought the food to the couch and sat down, and Sebastian followed with two glasses and a bottle of something homemade. It came in a lemonade bottle, so I was guessing juice from his grandfather's orchard.

He dimmed the lights on the way, which didn't help with the nerves.

On the outside, this looked like a romantic dinner date.

I wanted dates with him. After hiding for so long, I wanted everything I'd missed out on. Maybe even hand-holding and subtle ass-grabs at the store. I wanted to be up there on his wall.

"I wanna say the right thing. Do the right thing." He tucked into his meal and shook his head. "Can't fucking think near you."

I narrowed my eyes. What exactly was the right thing? I

119

didn't care about right and wrong. I wanted him to just be honest. Both with me and himself.

"Do you have any wine?" I asked. It might help. Thinking was overrated. That was how sober decisions were made.

He nodded with a dip of his chin and finished chewing on his way to the kitchen.

I forked up some lasagna and shoveled it into my mouth. He was weird about food. Knowing him, he wasn't gonna let me do anything if I didn't eat first, so I wanted to get it out of the way.

It was good. Soph's recipe. She put zucchini and Italian sausage in her lasagna too.

I managed to chow down three mouthfuls before Sebastian was back with two wineglasses and a bottle of red.

"Are you forcing yourself to eat?" His forehead creased.

I nodded, unafraid to be honest for once. "Too nervous to be hungry, but I know I gotta eat. Plus, this stunning ogre I know keeps fussin'."

"Stunning ogre." He snorted and sat down. "I'll take it, I guess." He poured me a glass and handed it over. "I don't suppose you wanna let the wine breathe—never mind."

Yeah, I was already guzzling it down.

"You've been nervous a lot lately, haven't you?" he murmured.

I nodded again, a bit more hesitant this time. I didn't know if this was chitchat or the first step toward something serious. Sooner or later, he had to give me his thoughts.

"That's why you said I wasn't so innocent," he concluded with a faint smile. "Because I've been making you feel this way?"

"Maybe." I cleared my throat and focused on my food. That hadn't been my best moment.

Two more big bites, and my food was almost gone. I stuffed my mouth with some salad too and washed it down with more wine. He couldn't complain anymore. I'd eaten. And if I ended up with a stomachache, it was on him.

Now I had a job to do. I had to convince him. I could tell he was on the fence, guarded, still processing. There was also a sense of wariness in his posture and in his eyes. He was as clueless as I was. Or as I had been. Not anymore. I knew what I wanted.

I still had his stereo system stored in my phone, so I went in and connected the device to my Bluetooth, then picked a playlist with slower country rock.

"You're up to something," he accused.

"Of course I am." I grabbed our plates and headed for the kitchen. He'd eaten less than I had, but he wasn't really hungry either. "I know you. You're trying to come up with a way to ask me to leave. You'll give me some spiel on how you need time to process everythin', and you'll keep comin' up with excuses. It wouldn't surprise me if your argument contains the words 'boundaries' and 'slow things down.'" I grimaced and made my way back to the living room. "I say, no thank you, sir. I'm done with the distance. I'm done with boundaries." More than that, I was done with him being mad at me. Near the bookcases at the other end of the living room, I picked up a bottle of bourbon and poured us two glasses. "It's time we do this my way, darlin'."

"What way is that?"

"Whatever way makes you forget you want me out of your life."

He sighed and accepted the drink. "I don't want you out of my life, Blake. If I did, you wouldn't be here."

"But you resent me," I said. "You wanna stay angry with me."

I took a sip of the bourbon and immediately had to take one more before I sat down too. Lord, it was amazing. Smooth, with a caramel aftertaste to soothe the spicy burn. "You know how to choose your bourbon."

He didn't reply.

I sat with my back against the armrest, wanting to face him fully, and pulled up one leg, resting my knee against the cushion.

It didn't escape my notice that he flicked a glance at my position. More accurately, that I had my legs parted. And it was why he couldn't think near me, right? The jury was still out where my personality was concerned, but at least I had one edge. He was inexplicably drawn to me physically. It was why our chemistry was off the charts in the bedroom. He was obsessed with me, and I was obsessed with him. And our brains —fuck me twice. They became one. As soon as he voiced a command, my body responded.

"I can take my sweats off if that makes me more likable," I offered. I wasn't even joking.

He chuckled tiredly into his drink. "I think the problem is I like you a little too much."

Finally, progress.

"But you're right," he continued. "I've been actively trying to stay angry to keep you at arm's length—possibly my area of expertise—and now I don't know how to go on. After everything you unloaded, I just..." He took a deep breath and released it, and I got a glimpse of his emotional fatigue. Perhaps because I could relate. "I feel like I've run out of steam."

Seeing him so wrung-out—maybe it was a victory in the end, because now we could get somewhere. Now he was willing to skip all the pretenses and listen. And talk. Properly. At the same time, it tugged at something in me. I wanted the bad to go away. I wanted to take it away from him.

I kinda knew where to start too.

"Do you have any snacks?" I asked and got off the couch.

Sebastian furrowed his brow and gestured his glass toward the kitchen. "Sure. The cupboard above the fridge where Teddy can't reach."

Clever. He knew my nephew.

While I was in the kitchen, I pulled a 180 and changed the topic entirely. "So how's Lily doin' these days? You think she'll be an indoor or outdoor cat?"

Growing up on a ranch, I'd always been surrounded by cats, but they were part of the workforce. It hadn't been encouraged to treat them like pets, much to my sister's devastation as a child. According to Dad, coddling kittens made them weak and lazy.

"I'm not sure yet," Sebastian replied. "I've let her explore the porch now that the protective netting doesn't stand in her way. She'll jump up on the railing, but that's about it. When Mischa huffs at her, she'll come inside."

That was cute as fuck. Mischa was a daddy in his own right.

Fuck yeah, Sebastian had Ruffles. The original flavor, too, because there was no reason to mess with perfection.

"You have Ruffles." I popped the bag and poured the chips into a bowl.

"You inhaled three bags last time you were in town."

"And now you keep them around for me. I'm touched, darlin'." I actually was.

"Don't read into it," he muttered.

I grinned to myself and grabbed a box of Milk Duds too.

"Can I ask what you're doing, Blake? What's your game here? You switched gears, and now you're all...I don't know, casual."

"Yeah, I think that's what we need." I returned to the living room. "For once."

Sebastian lifted a brow. "Casual—for once?"

"Yup." I sat down next to him and kissed his cheek. "It

123

would be a first for us, wouldn't it? We were never casual before."

He glanced at me, and I was ready to clear the confusion and weary frustration from his expression.

"I want casual evenings with the man I was never casual with," I said. "I'm not gonna split when shit gets real this time, Sebastian. Real is all I want—with you. So you can take some time to wrap your head around that while I work that smallest TV known to man." I swore my little flat-screen in the RV was bigger than Sebastian's. His couldn't be more than twenty-eight inches. "It should be illegal," I grumbled to myself and picked up the remote. "Now, I'm not sayin' you need a seventy-inch. When it comes to TVs, I'm no size queen—it's gotta fit the livin' room, and it depends on the distance between the screen and the couch. But this...? This is a joke."

After shutting off the music, I restarted the fishing show I watched with Teddy. Season 1, Episode 1, go.

"You wear me out, Kidd." Sebastian sighed and sank lower on the couch. With his bourbon in his hand, resting on his thigh, he planted his feet on the table and crossed them at the ankles.

"I'm ready to wear you down too." I draped my arm along the back of the couch and kissed the side of his head.

He peered up at me. "Spell it out for me. How can you talk about being real when you're only here temporarily? If I weren't completely drained and too fucking weak to resist you, I'd kick you out right about now."

Oh Christ. He still thought I was here just for the duration of building Soph and Dylan's house?

"That's another assumption." I eased my fingers between his brows to smooth out the worry wrinkle. "I'm not goin' anywhere. I'm moving to Washington. Soph is too integrated. Y'all need some fresh Southern meat who can bitch about your weather."

Sebastian exhaled a shaky laugh and closed his eyes. "Tell me you're serious." When he opened them again, everything became so damn clear. We'd traveled the exact same journey, struggled with the same feelings, and we couldn't fight it any longer.

"I'm serious." I dipped down and brushed my lips to his. "Lord knows you've owned my ass since summer. Now you get to own the rest of me too. If you want."

He smiled into the kiss and teased the tip of his tongue around mine. "I want."

And the crowd went wild.

Kidding aside, holy fuck, the relief was unreal.

"Yeah?"

"You have no idea." He pecked me twice more before inching away again. "You've put me through the goddamn wringer. I was already caving before today. You probably could've promised me the same deal as this summer—with the same outcome—and I would've gone through with it."

I knew the feeling.

"Same here." I pressed my lips to the top of his head and breathed him in. It was insane how quickly my body adjusted and relaxed, but my mind couldn't grasp it yet. "You always smell so damn good." It was a combination of his cologne, the ocean, regular soap, and the shampoo he used.

Sebastian hummed and shifted closer until he could rest the side of his face on my chest. "So do you." He took another sip of his bourbon, then set it down on the table and pulled his tee over his head. Much better.

"You forgot your jeans," I noted.

He grinned and nipped at my nipple. "I don't know if you remember, but I go commando."

As if I would forget. "That's why I said something, hon."

He chuckled and shook his head, and then the fucker left

me. He stood up. "I'll go put on some sweats. I want that casual evening you promised."

"I'll be right here." I couldn't stop smiling, and I watched him walk away. That ass of his—man. His whole body was a work of art. Broad shoulders, solid frame, just the right amount of definition.

When it was just me in the room, not counting the boys and...wherever Lily was hiding now, I released a breath and lolled my head against the back cushion.

I was gonna end up on that wall, so help me God. Sebastian and I were gonna be in pictures together. *Like a couple.* A thought that was both intimidating and exhilarating. I couldn't fuck this up. If I did, I knew I would lose the best thing that could ever happen to me.

The anxiousness had morphed into softer flutters.

They were a lot more stomach-friendly. They even added to the bizarre joy.

I threw a handful of chips into my mouth and got comfortable with the bowl on my lap and the bourbon in my hand. Feet up on the table. Tomorrow, I just might buy Sebastian a bigger TV so shit could really get perfect.

This was it, right? No more surprises. No more *bad* surprises.

The next time we argued, it would be as a couple.

I was almost looking forward to that. As long as rough make-up sex followed.

When I got home, hopefully not until tomorrow, I was gonna have to google some shit.

"I'm in my first relationship. How do I not screw up?"

"Did you mean: I screwed up my first relationship?"

"Fuck you, Google," I whispered under my breath. "Fuck you."

I was finished with my bourbon and most of the chips by the

time Sebastian came down the stairs again.

He'd showered. His sweats clung low on his hips, and the muscles in his arms and across his torso looked ripped as he pulled back his hair into his usual hippie-bun.

"My Washington hippie." I smirked. "I don't think I've ever seen you with your hair down, outside the bathroom."

Once in the ocean, only when he redid the thing with the rubber band.

"I look ridiculous in short hair, so you'll have to deal with this." He collapsed next to me and grabbed a couple chips. "Did your appetite return while I was gone?"

"Maybe," I laughed. "Funny how that works."

He gripped my chin and angled me for a quick kiss. "You and me. Can you believe it?"

"I actually can't," I chuckled. "I'm giddier than a kid on Christmas, but my brain can't process it."

"Sounds about right." He smiled and kissed me again, then shifted into his previous position—feet on the table, his shoulders low enough for me to put my arm around him, which I fucking did. "We'll have to be patient with each other." He gave my leg a squeeze. "Your first relationship and my first healthy one—I hope. Christ, we're fucked."

I laughed. "Yeah, probably."

He hummed and turned his face to kiss my chest. "I've missed hearing you laugh like that."

I'd missed everything about him.

"I think I'm fairly easy to be with, though," he said pensively. "I have three rules. No major lies, zero tolerance for betrayal and cheating, and no forcing me to watch football. Oh, wait—four rules. You gotta take my side when Soph and I fight."

Yikes. The first two were a nonissue. "I feel like those last two rules are just gonna set us up for failure." But hey, I could compromise. Compromises were part of being in a relationship, according to Soph and Google. "I'll agree to the last one if you take *my* side when I'm the one fighting with her."

Sebastian sucked his teeth. "Fine."

I was good with that for now. A lot had already happened today, and I wasn't sure I could cram more information into my skull.

Well, there was one thing. Only because I didn't wanna get it wrong. "Lemme get this straight. I can lie and tell you I think it's perfectly reasonable to have a bike and a four-wheeler but no actual car, but I wouldn't lie about anything that might hurt—"

"Hey." He frowned up at me. "It's perfectly reasonable to have a Harley and a four-wheeler."

I stared at him.

He wasn't serious, was he? He could only take Teddy places when it was warm enough to use the ATV, and they couldn't go very far. He had to borrow my truck or Soph and Dylan's car.

"Sure." I kissed him on the forehead. "Let's watch some TV. I have so many shows to corrupt you with." Because who could forget that Sebastian had said he wasn't a big fan of watching TV.

No man was perfect.

CHAPTER
9

That night, we put each other back together. He asked me to stay, and we spent the night in and out of sleep, waking up here and there just to talk and be close to each other.

We still had some scars to tend to.

The summer's thin top sheet had been replaced by a thick duvet, and I couldn't imagine leaving my spot. My head on his chest, his fingers trailing up and down my arm, his steady breaths...

This was what peace felt like.

"I remember when you said there was no harm in getting to know each other," he murmured. "It was all just fun."

I remembered that too. "I'm not always a genius," I muttered drowsily. "How was I supposed to know you were gonna turn me into a person with actual feelings?"

He trembled with a silent chuckle.

We fell back asleep shortly after, and when I woke up again, we'd shifted in our sleep so he was spooning me.

I could get used to this.

"Sebastian," I whispered.

"Mm."

"I thought of another rule."

He yawned and stretched a little, which became highly

distracting when he gripped my hip and pressed his pre-morning wood against my ass.

"You're bordering on high-maintenance now, Blake. How many are you at?"

Only six. One, he had to let me buy him a proper TV. Two, he had to watch TV with me once a week. Three, we had to do romantic shit every now and then because I had never experienced that. Four, I was expanding on Soph's rule about football on Thanksgiving to include a breakfast game. Sebastian had to come with us to that sports bar at least once a year so he could see what the fuss was about. Five, a lot of sex. A lot of it. Six, no more rubbers. Just oil or lube, depending on where we fucked, and we had to be packin' wherever we went.

"Just one more," I said. "Let's install heaters on the porch and on the balcony so we don't freeze to death."

One of the hottest things I'd ever seen was Sebastian sitting naked on the sofa out there on the balcony, a drink in one hand, a cigar in the other. And it was a travesty to limit that to the very brief Washington summer.

"I wanna sit at your feet and service your cock when you smoke a cigar," I finished.

"Jesus," he whispered, tightening his hold on my hip. "I was ready to argue until you said that."

Great, I win.

"So it's a deal?" I asked.

"It's a deal." He kissed my neck, then disappeared to grab something. I heard him opening the nightstand drawer. Please let it be oil. We'd waited long enough. "Now I have a rule of my own," he said. "Every now and then, I wanna sleep while I'm balls deep in your ass."

My ass clenched with want. Fuck yeah, I could only imagine how that kind of frustration would turn me into a greedy whore for him.

"Sometimes I'll wake up needing you right then and there," he went on. I felt his arm moving behind me, hopefully because he was slicking up his cock. "And you won't make a sound unless something's wrong. Not a damn sound. Those nights, you'll just be my toy. I'll empty myself and go back to sleep."

"Holy fuck." I exhaled through a shiver and pressed against his cock. "Yeah, I'm game. Best rule ever."

"And you're a fantasy come true," he laughed softly. "I've never been able to go all in like this with anyone. Most of my fetishes have stayed in my head."

"Well, now you have me." I hugged my pillow, smug as shit. "I told you from the beginnin', darlin'. Use me however you want in the sack."

"I will." He didn't say anything else. Instead, he pushed the head of his cock between my ass cheeks, then drove forward in a single thrust.

I sucked in a breath as the intense burn spread, and I couldn't help but clamp down on him, which only made the pain worse.

I groaned into the pillow.

"Hurt for me, baby." He leaned over me and trapped my earlobe between his teeth. "Those first few seconds when I take you—or when I shove my cock down your throat—I want to own every inch of your body and mind. I'll be the only thing that exists for you."

Oh God.

"You are," I rasped.

"Good boy." He kissed my shoulder and wrapped his arm around my middle. "Now go back to sleep."

My eyes flashed open.

He was the goddamn *devil.*

I woke up to him fucking me.

It messed with my head, because I couldn't imagine him being able to do a whole lot without my noticing, but it was still a full-on fuck I roused to, and he was hard as a rock. He hitched an arm under my leg, too, and angled himself to take me deeper.

Most of the discomfort was gone, and the fantasy itself slammed enough lust into me that all I wanted was more. But I gave him what he wanted. Nothing. Not a sound. I didn't move either, even as my own cock grew painfully hard and demanded attention.

He wasn't quiet or careful about anything. His groans and heavy breaths filled the air and turned me on beyond belief.

"No—go back downstairs, Echo. Daddy's busy."

Jesus fucking Christ. My face suddenly felt like it was on fire, and I didn't really understand it. We'd shooed away the boys before, but this was different somehow.

It was so hot that I didn't know what to do with myself.

It took all my self-control not to move when he wrapped his fingers around my cock.

"Look at that. My sleeping beauty gets off on being used as a come dumpster."

I gnashed my teeth to keep from whimpering like a needy preteen.

"Not a single sound." He kissed my shoulder before pulling out from me, and then he rolled me onto my back. A beat later, my cock disappeared into his warm, wet mouth, and I had absolutely no outlet for my frustration. I wanted to shout, curse, jackhammer my cock into his mouth, and beg to come. Instead, I kept it all bottled up inside and fisted the sheets as discreetly as I could.

As he sucked me off, he pressed his thumb inside my ass, as a teasing reminder of something much larger he was hopefully pushing in later.

"I missed this beautiful cock," he murmured, licking the underside all the way up till he could wrap his lips around the head. Simultaneously, he moved his thumb in my ass in caressing strokes that messed with my mind further. Like a dirty little *There, there, I've got you.* "Mmm, I forgot how much you come even before you get off. Your cock is a needy come slut just like you."

An unsteady breath slipped between my lips, and my whole body tensed up.

It felt too good. If there was one thing a guy could feel, it was whether the one giving head was really into it. And he was. He swallowed around the head, coated me with his tongue, drank every drop, and shoved me toward the brink with long, firm movements. Then faster and faster. Cheeks hollowed out— God, I felt the soft flesh of his cheeks hugging my cock, creating a tight sleeve that I sank deeper and deeper into.

My breathing hitched right before my orgasm hit me, and I hoped it was all the warning he needed, because then I was coming. I screwed my eyes shut, stopped breathing, and clenched my teeth so hard I might have crushed my molars.

I imploded with pleasure.

My heart thundered.

And he gave me no time to recover whatsoever. I was still riding the high when he flipped me over, his cock finding me fast, and started fucking me into the mattress.

He came within minutes, and I couldn't describe the sensation. Being used like that, being trapped by my own euphoria, unable to move and make a sound, then ending up as his personal wastebasket. I didn't care if it made me a pervert, but if this was what I had to look forward to, I was gonna die a happy man.

At five in the morning, we found ourselves on the balcony upstairs, cocooned by blankets and a duvet, chugging his home-made apple and pineapple juice and eating lasagna leftovers and bread.

I'd spotted my bed head in the glass door earlier. It was impressive.

"Do we really need heaters?" he pondered.

"Yes." I dragged a piece of bread through the tomato sauce and crammed it into my mouth. I was the one who'd woken him up, and as soon as I'd mentioned being starving, he'd jumped into action. He definitely had a weird thing about making sure I ate.

Safe to say, my appetite had returned.

"You can't honestly say you're cold," he said with an expression full of doubt.

"I'm not a yeti like you, darlin'." I spoke with my mouth full of delicious food. "It's warm under the covers, but think about it. I wanna be able to see you if we're gonna get down and dirty out here."

Speaking of, a porch light would be nice too. There wasn't a single source of light at the moment, not counting the pale, predawn glow over the mountains behind us.

"Thank you for a fantastic meal." I wiped my mouth and set the plate on the table. "Do you happen to have a lot of yard sales in this town?"

"Interesting change of topic." Sebastian leaned forward and set aside his plate too. "Yeah, I wanna say they're fairly common. I think there's an organized sale event in Westslope every Sunday—but it could be seasonal. People pop their trunks full of shit in the parking lot outside the strip mall."

I'd have to look it up. That was perfect, just what I was looking for.

"My obvious question is *why*?" He nudged me and grinned a little.

"Well, the guesthouse will be ready next week," I replied. "If I'm gonna invite my beast over for dinner, I'll need cookware. Yard sales are the best places to find that. Can't beat a cast-iron skillet or Dutch oven that's already been used for twenty years. Nine times out of ten, they just need a new handle and some love."

Sebastian dropped his chin onto my shoulder and pressed a smiling kiss to my neck. "Your beast, huh? I'm sensing a theme. You've called me Shrek, an ogre, a beast, and a yeti."

I chuckled and nudged him back so I could get comfortable in his arms. "Consider those terms little reminders of my appreciation for your size. Both you and your horse cock."

He burst out a laugh that made me grin.

"I like being your beast." He hugged me to him and closed the duvet around us. "You wanna get some more sleep?"

I nodded. I could've fallen asleep right there if my feet weren't poking out from all the warm layers. "Yeah, my toes are freezin'."

I got up reluctantly and quickly kicked it up a notch, because as soon as I was out of the duvet, it was so cold that my balls wanted to crawl back into my body.

"Jesus, Mary, and Joseph, that ain't right!" I hurried back inside the bedroom and threw the duvet onto the bed.

Half expecting Sebastian to find my outburst funny and possibly too dramatic, I was a little disappointed when he didn't react at all.

He seemed distracted by something.

"You okay?" I got under the covers and sat down on the mattress.

"Yeah, I was just thinking." He set our dishes on his little bar cart for now, then joined me in bed. "I owe you an apology too. No matter the reason, no matter how hurt I was, I've treated you horribly since you got back." He found my hand under the duvet and threaded our fingers together. "When Soph started defending you, I became livid—even when I saw with my own eyes that you were doing everything to redeem yourself."

"Sebastian, you don't have to apologize for anything. I deserved—"

"Two wrongs don't make a right," he interjected. "And the thing is, I knew exactly when my words packed a punch. It made me sick to see you get hurt. To see that *I* was hurting you."

This was quickly becoming uncomfortable because I didn't wanna think back on that time anymore. I'd been miserable, just like he had.

"But shit's good now." I scooted closer and nudged him back against the pillows. "Water under the bridge and all that."

He smiled faintly and gathered his arms around me. "There's one more thing. You're not gonna like it."

Urgh. My brain instantly registered the subtle humor in his tone, but fuck if my stomach didn't drop and fill with dread.

"When I found out you'd skipped town," he said soberly, "I told Sophia that the biscuits you made me weren't very good."

I closed my eyes and dropped my forehead to his chest. Oh, he thought he was being funny. I felt him shake with silent laughter, all while I was thanking God it wasn't anything serious. I needed help.

"You *asshole*," I groaned.

The fucker didn't stop laughing. He threw the duvet over us, and he fucking howled. Which eventually turned into wheezing giggles, and...well, who the fuck could stay mad at that? He had the richest, most masculine voice, and hearing it dissolve into a giggle fit was something else.

I couldn't help but chuckle.

Pushing away the duvet again, I got a look at his gorgeous

face and the stunning smile he was sporting, and it was just everything to me. He was really happy.

"But you only said that 'cause you were mad, right?" I had to make sure. "You had four of them and kept the rest for leftovers."

It'd been a good evening. I'd cooked for him, real Southern home cookin', and he'd had three servings of Nana Margaret's roast beef, served with mashed potatoes, roasted carrots, green beans, and my buttermilk-cheddar biscuits.

"No, I promise—" Sebastian reached down and grabbed my ass. "I'm a big fan of your biscuits. The ones you bake too."

Good. It was the only thing I knew how to bake, and it was kinda my claim to fame.

I dumped my laundry in the back of the truck and fastened Percy and Oppy's carrier, then made my way back to where Sebastian waited in the doorway. "Remind me again of why I gotta leave?"

He squinted for the sun and pulled off a sleepy smile. "I gotta head up to see Pops."

Right. And then he had work tonight. And tomorrow night, and the evening after that too.

I'd earned my break from work, but time was beginning to run out. No matter how frugally I tended to live, I had to find a job soon. Starting my own business was pretty appealing, though that would have to come down the road.

"You know what you could do?" He dipped his fingers into my jeans and tugged me into his embrace. "Come by the restaurant tonight, and I'll have dinner waiting for you."

An offer I couldn't refuse. "I'll be there. I have a feelin' my second visit will be different from the first."

"I sure hope so." He rumbled a chuckle and kissed me. "You pissed me off the other day—the constant hollering of 'Bartender!'"

My grin turned sheepish. "I was jealous of that mother-fucker you were with."

He hummed. "I already texted him. Said it wasn't a good time to explore anything—even friendship—and I didn't wanna give him false hope."

"Thank you." I squeezed him to me and dropped a kiss to his shoulder. "You're all mine, right?"

"Hey." He cupped the back of my neck and made me look him in the eye. "What you said last night—we were never casual. There wasn't a snowball's chance in hell I was gonna be able to move on that soon. So I wanna say it's been just you and me since this summer."

Good. Fuck, that was good. And felt good to hear. "Same here." I leaned in for a quick kiss. "The jitters get worse when I think about people getting in our way or me fucking things up."

"Those are the bad jitters." He scratched my neck and up in my hair, instantly giving me a moment's peace. I closed my eyes because it felt so nice. "We'll work on those together, yeah? We're both new at this. We'll be careful in the beginning until we find solid ground to land on. How's that?"

I smiled lazily and forced my eyes to open again. "You say all the right things, Wilder. Except when you tell me to leave."

He chuckled and rested his forehead to mine. "Believe me, baby, I wish I didn't have to."

Sweet Jesus, the way he made me feel. I rode out the shiver of utter bliss and gave him one more kiss. "I'll see you tonight."

He nodded as I stepped back. "Bring an overnight bag. Which reminds me—" He went into the hallway, missing out on my cheesy grin—something that was probably for the best—and returned with a key. "Make it a late dinner and drop off your boys and your things here before you come to the restaurant. Then you can stay until we close."

I liked that idea. I accepted the key and felt like maybe that was significant. At least for me.

"It looks like it's gonna be a nice day, so I might walk to work."

I felt my forehead wrinkle. "You're gonna walk all the way to the marina?"

He laughed through his nose. "It's not that far—and I like walking."

Yeah, right. He just wanted to drive my truck home later.

"Don't hitch rides from strangers, darlin'." I offered a two-finger wave and reluctantly turned back to the truck. "Feel free to send me cute texts today. I think I'm gonna take it easy and check out yard sales and some stores online. I'mma need a sturdy bed in the guesthouse."

"A four-poster would be cool," he mentioned. "I got ropes."

I grinned and jumped into my truck. "Such a flirt, Wilder."

He smirked. "See you tonight, Kidd."

I could hardly wait.

CHAPTER
10

O ver the next several days, I balanced my obsession for being with Sebastian with finishing the guesthouse.

Nine hours to go, no time to waste. I was showing Soph this house tonight when she got back from Seattle with Teddy, so help me.

Hardwood floors, done. Spotlights installed in the ceiling, done. Paint job, done.

Dylan was coming over this afternoon to assemble the bed and the rest of the furniture while I made final touches, such as the kitchen bar's heavy oak top that needed to be resized and treated. But hell, this place already looked good. It had everything a guesthouse needed. A small bedroom, just big enough for a queen bed, two nightstands, and a built-in closet. A bathroom with the basics. A tiny kitchen with a bar that seated two. The living room area, which took up most of the downstairs space, would have two small couches and one cushy chair, from where I could catch a game on the fifty-inch flat-screen about to be mounted on the wall.

My morning project consisted of adding shelves to the space underneath the narrow staircase that led to the sleeping loft. I'd already wrestled six twin beds up there. Sebastian had installed the lighting yesterday, so the only thing missing was shit Soph would be in charge of. Linens, covers, pillows. Essentially, it was gonna be an area to stash David's kids when they visited.

The terrorizing toddlers could crash on the couches, while Mama and Daddy took the bedroom.

I grabbed the level from my tool belt and checked to make sure the next shelf was...nope. I took the pen from behind my ear and made a new mark about two millimeters below the old one. There we go.

With such limited space, I hadn't wanted to waste any room on extra closets. I'd think creatively instead, something I knew my sister would appreciate. Hence turning the staircase into a shelving unit with drawers and cabinets. Even the kitchen bar had secret compartments, and there would be a dresser by the door too. That was plenty.

My phone rang right before I was about to pick up the drill, so I stalked over to the kitchen bar and hoped to see my new contractor's number on the screen. Construction jobs came and went fast, and I needed confirmation that we could begin building in March—before the permits expired.

Alas, it was David calling me.

"Howdy, big brother. Mind if you make it quick? I'm waitin' for an important call." I trapped the phone between my shoulder and cheek and went over to the coffeemaker to refill my mug.

"No problem, this won't take long," he responded. "I spoke to Soph already. Melissa and I would like to have y'all over for Christmas."

Oh. That gave me a pause. I scratched my chest and flicked a glance downward, only to grimace at the sheer amount of sawdust stuck to my tee. On a normal day, it wouldn't bother me for crap, but I was meeting up with Sebastian for lunch in an hour, and I didn't have time to change.

"I take it Soph and Dylan accepted?" I asked.

I didn't know the protocol here. Sebastian had his own family. I didn't know if they'd already made plans—or if we were supposed to spend the holidays separately. I sure as heck hoped not.

"Yes, they were with Dylan's family last Christmas," David said. "Mel and I are basically stealing Mom and Dad's celebration."

I chuckled and took a sip of my coffee. It felt kind of good to have reached the stage where we could joke about something revolving around our folks. A pang of sorrow could hit me at the most random moments, but the support of Soph and David had made all the difference. Mom was going to keep pretending as if nothing had happened, and they weren't going to play along.

"I'd love to be there," I admitted. "I'm just...sort of in a plus-one situation now, so I reckon I gotta talk to him first."

"Soph told me." David had a smile in his tone, and it felt good. "We're very happy for you, Blake. Don't fuck it up."

I let out a laugh. It wasn't often my brother cussed. "I'm doing my best. But according to Soph, we look ridiculously love-sick. We didn't even tell her that we worked everythin' out. She took one glance at us and knew."

David laughed softly. "I hope I'll get to see you both for the holidays, then. Let me know as soon as possible, please."

"Will do. Give Melissa and the kids my love." We wrapped up the call, and I took another swig of my coffee and checked my messages. There was a text from Sebastian.

You hunt, right?

I hesitated as I mulled over my answer. I couldn't say yes outright because it'd been a couple years now. I'd considered myself out of the game for the time being once Rosie couldn't handle the long treks anymore. On the other hand, I missed it. And a former avid hunter couldn't move to Washington without taking advantage of the best part of the state, could he?

I'd like to get back to it, but it's been a while. Why?

Maybe he wanted me to go with his pops as some kind of chaperone. The last few days, Sebastian and his sister had been trying to get their grandfather to realize it wasn't safe for him to head out alone. The old man couldn't walk up the stairs in his own home, but he was gonna go out and shoot deer in the mountains?

I'd have to say I sided with Sebastian. It seemed a little too risky.

Sebastian's reply popped up with a picture that made my eyebrows lift. It was of a beautiful dog, a mix of some sort, possible German shepherd and a Lab. Maybe something else too, because the dog appeared a tad smaller, more slender, and its coat was a dark, rich coffee-brown color.

One of Pops's hunting buddies' grandsons recently had a baby who's turned out to be allergic to dogs. The dog's name is Nala. She's two years old, trained in blood tracking, small game retrieval, and recovery. So it goes without saying she needs a new owner who can give her a life in the field. I told Pops I'd talk to you, but they're gonna need a quick answer.

That was fine, because I had a quick response.

Let me meet with the owner and Nala. But the answer is fuck yes.

I didn't dare hope too much. This kind of thing wasn't too uncommon, and I'd seen shit go sideways before. When selecting an adult dog, there had to be chemistry, even more so with a working dog or one trained in hunting. But sweet Jesus, something just clicked when I looked at the photo again. And it didn't have so much to do with Nala specifically, but with the fact that I was incredibly ready to find a new four-legged companion. It was time. Spending my nights with Sebastian, who had that tight bond with Mischa, didn't help.

Sebastian answered again.

I had a feeling. :-) I think she can be great for you. I'll call Pops right away. See you soon.

I scrubbed a hand over my mouth and tried to withhold the smile. No, dang it, I wasn't gonna get ahead of myself yet.

Today was Sebastian's last shift at the restaurant for a while. His boss was back from his vacation, so there'd be a new schedule coming out in which Sebastian would return to occasional nights and weekends. He was happy with that, but I was gonna miss our lunches.

After another poor attempt at brushing sawdust off my tee, I opened the door to the restaurant and stepped into the warmth.

These little dates we'd started having at the restaurant, especially if one was during a lunch shift, messed with my head. Work lunches were grunt affairs, and you looked like a troll coming straight from a work site, utility pants still on, and you had the dirty tees and steel-toe boots. But I was raised to dress up, smell nice, and be clean for dates.

I didn't tick any of those boxes right now.

Sebastian appeared from the dining section with two plates and a sexy smile. "Right on time."

"Of course."

He led the way to the seating area by the bar, which was empty at this hour.

"Have a seat. I'll get you a beer." He pressed a quick kiss to my temple before he was off again.

I did love meeting up with him like this in the middle of the day, though. Maybe we could find a way to do it when he worked his other jobs too.

I took a seat and unfolded the napkin across my thigh. The food smelled fantastic as always. He'd given me the crab ravioli with lemon butter and roasted vegetables again, because it was freaking heaven, something that couldn't have gone unnoticed last time.

They had a great chef here, that was for certain.

Sebastian came back with two ice waters and a beer.

"How will your schedule look when you go back to your regular job?" I asked. As far as I knew, he was at it again starting Monday. Every morning, he'd drive around town and pick up special needs children and take them to school. Same story when school was out and the kids had to go home again. And if I wasn't mistaken, he had pickups in between too, when he drove kids to doctors' appointments, care groups, and activities.

"I'll work seven thirty to four every day," he replied, tucking into his halibut. I'd tried that too, but it wasn't as good as the ravioli. "Tuesdays to Thursdays will be busier because I'll have a few hours at the Quad after work too."

"Oh. Can I come see you at the Quad? Will you be able to meet up for lunch here and there?"

He glanced up from his food and smiled. "Yes to both."

Thank fuck. "Good. I've gotten used to getting a dose in the middle of the day."

He chuckled and squeezed my hand over the table. "You don't know how hooked I am on what we have now. We don't have to hold back."

"That was half the anxiety last time." I remembered thinking I had to make sure I wasn't too interested or acted too affectionate, for fear he'd think I was *crossing lines*. "But now... things are almost too good. I'm waitin' for the other shoe to drop sometimes. You know what I mean?"

"Yeah, it's weird. I guess that's our history talking."

True. We both came from backgrounds where shit went south one way or another.

On the flipside, every relationship began because the previous ones had failed.

There was something comforting about that fact. It just made us normal.

"Circling back to the Quad," I said, forking up another piece of ravioli. "When I picked you up the other day, I saw you had a bulletin board near the entrance with a bunch of sign-ups for classes and whatnot."

He nodded and shoveled some food into his mouth. "We encourage the kids to learn basic stuff like budgeting, cooking, cleaning... It's a place for small businesses to recruit holiday workers too."

"That's cool. Do you put together those classes yourselves?" I asked.

"Sometimes. Maggie runs a cooking class every month. Dominic teaches self-defense every now and then, I've done a few classes for those who don't know how to swim, and the volunteers who're teachers by day run their own tutoring service. Things like that. Many kids are also at the age where they're getting ready to take their driver's license exams, so we try to stay up-to-date if anyone needs help with the written tests."

In other words, this could be a good opportunity for me to let my feet grow roots. I wanted to be part of a community. More than that, I admired Sebastian for the work he did, and he was a good inspiration.

I cleared my throat and sat back in my seat. "So...if someone were to offer a class to learn, say, simple carpentry, that could be a good idea?"

He was busy chewing, but his eyes filled with enough

warmth for me to know I was on the right path. "Good idea is an understatement." He washed down the rest of his food with a swig of water, and then he grabbed my hands on the table. "That's the kind of initiative that makes me wanna..." He trailed off, much to my sudden frustration, and he glanced at something behind me. Made him wanna *what*? "It's my boss," he said quietly.

Oh, he was coming over.

"Sorry to interrupt your lunch," the man muttered distract-edly. He was flipping through some printouts.

I hadn't really thought about Sebastian's boss before, but I supposed he looked like what I would've expected. Rugged, maybe a few years older than us, judging by the silver in his scruff. He happened to be handsome as hell too, and he was walking with a limp.

"I'm putting Niko on more kitchen duty," he said. "Would you mind covering one of his evening shifts at the bar? I thought I'd divide his hours between the rest of you."

"Yeah, no problem at all." Sebastian seemed pleased to get more hours. "If possible, I'd like to avoid Friday and Saturday, but..."

"No sweat. You're my only bartender who doesn't mind working Sundays. I'll pencil you in. Thanks, Sebastian." He made a move to leave when Sebastian spoke again.

"Hey, weren't you and Gray searching for someone who could help you expand your farm or something?"

The man cocked his head. "We need an extra hand for a few projects next spring, yeah. Why?"

Sebastian nodded at me. "You should talk to Blake. He's worked all over the field—construction, renovations, you name it."

That seemed to pique the man's interest, and he extended a hand to me.

"Darius Quinn."

I shook it firmly. "Blake Kidd—nice to meet you, sir. I actually have a card here somewhere..." I patted my pockets, all fucking six of them. When it came to work, one had to be prepared. There, found it. "I grew up on a ranch and was put to work before I could crawl, so whatever you might need on a farm, I'm sure I've got experience."

He grinned faintly and eyed the card before pocketing it. "Good to know. I'll definitely get in touch with you. We'll probably wanna get started right after the last frost. One farm, a million projects."

"It never ends," I chuckled in agreement.

Sebastian and I were left alone again a beat later, and I told him to feel free to pimp me out for work any day of the week.

"I'm just collecting things that tie you to Washington so you can't leave."

Behind the joke, I sensed a little bit of truth—or worry—and it was up to me to fix that.

I wasn't going anywhere.

"I've never been so damn happy before. I'm stayin' put." I dragged a ravioli through the buttery sauce and stuck it into my mouth. "Your boss seems nice, by the way."

"Yeah, he's great." Sebastian had finished his food, so he leaned forward and rested his forearms on the table. "He and his boyfriend live up in the woods with their two kids." That explained the name Gray. "They run their own little homestead farm—self-reliance and all that. Kinda the dream life, don't you think?"

I took a swallow of beer and wondered what he meant by that. He wanted to live in the woods? I wouldn't mind that. The woods were hunting grounds. I couldn't say I was sold on running a farm, though. Ranches and farms were the same fucking thing in that there was always too much to do. When you fixed one fence, another one broke.

"You wanna buy a farm and go off the grid?"

He laughed under his breath and shook his head. "No, and I don't wanna adopt kids either. Being with you has just made me more interested in seeing what the future might look like." He paused and checked his watch, perhaps to see how much he had left of his break. "All right—the truth. Pops is finally thinking about retiring in the next year or two, and he asked me the other day if taking over the orchard is something I would consider."

That made much more sense.

"What did you tell him?" I wondered.

Now that he'd mentioned it, I saw the appeal in thinking ahead—in making plans together. Because plans indicated we wanted to spend that future by each other's side.

"I didn't say a whole lot," he admitted. "On the one hand, I always loved his place in the woods. I grew up there. I followed him around as a kid and absorbed his little experiments with seeds, soils, and pollination, and I've worked there as an adult."

"And on the other hand...?"

He smiled ruefully. "On the other hand, I can't imagine leaving the beach house."

Yeah, I could see that struggle. One part of him wanted to do the work and settle down with a business, a legacy, and build a home. The other part of him was perfectly content in the beach house where the dogs could run around, where he was close to his beloved ocean, and where he had very little mainte-nance to worry about.

Knowing him, he'd also considered how taking over the orchard could help others. Sebastian's grandfather had survived the modernization and digitalization of businesses; he remained popular despite other corporations that imported cheaper prod-ucts and ran their operations from massive sites. In short, the

Wilder orchard was still thriving. It was worth investing and believing in. So I could imagine Sebastian would be able to provide jobs in the spring, summer, and fall.

It made me confused the more I thought about it. I didn't see the issue.

It was my turn to lean forward and rest my arms on the table, like some uncivilized heathen, as my mother would say. "I think I'm missin' something'," I said. "You don't have a mortgage, so why couldn't you keep both? The beach house is your home, and the orchard would be a place to work and run a business."

He nodded slowly and raked his teeth briefly over his bottom lip. "It's just a big commitment for one man. Pops's house needs fixing—he's spent the past thirty years doing temporary repairs because he doesn't have the time. He's always out wandering the fields along the river."

I'd never been up there, but I was curious. "How big's the orchard?"

"About ten acres," he replied. "It's tiny in comparison to most others."

Still, ten acres with barely any employees? That was one of the things I recalled from this summer. Sebastian often worried about his pops because he only had seven or eight part-time workers around.

"How many acres is your ranch?" he asked.

"Oh, uh..." I chuckled. "Little over four hundred?" I went on when he let out a low whistle. "But we have horses and cattle. It doesn't really compare to a ten-acre orchard heavy with production."

"I suppose."

Okay, here was the thing. Sebastian was hesitating because he was right; it would be a big commitment for one man. I, however, saw opportunities everywhere. The property was big enough to run a second and third operation. Hell, I could have a business based there. What it boiled down to was those future goals and whether we planned together or separately.

Or he's feeling you out, moron.

My head snapped up at that thought. Could that be it? Was he testing the waters?

I had news for him in that case, and I'd promised myself—and him—to be upfront with my intentions. As best as I could, anyway. I didn't have balls of steel, and sometimes I had to let ideas and wishes simmer a little.

Not for this. I knew what I wanted.

"You wouldn't have to be alone, though," I mentioned. "I mean—I'm hoping you won't be."

It was as endearing as it was rewarding to see the flash of hopefulness spark in his eyes, the green becoming clearer and warmer. Go me, I'd gotten that one right. And it was comforting to know I wasn't the only one fumbling at times.

Another thought struck me, and I couldn't help but smile. "Was this why you mentioned how your boss and his partner live?" Because Sebastian wanted to know if that was something I wanted?

He cleared his throat and broke eye contact for a moment, only to recover with a huffed chuckle and a self-deprecating smirk. "You're still my biggest weakness, Blake. I'm terrified to lose you, and I don't wanna rush too far ahead before you're ready."

My chest tightened with the strangest emotions, both uncomfortable and exciting. Nerves, anxiousness, protective-ness, *love...*

Fucking hell. How I just *knew.* The feeling was wholly unfamiliar yet so easily recognizable.

I needed some contact for this, so I moved our plates aside and gathered his hands in mine. "Since we apparently share the exact same fears, how about we put all our cards on the table? I don't mind being your biggest weakness—it's an ego boost and a half, to be honest. But it goes both ways. You're my biggest weakness too."

That earned me a slight twist of his lips, and a pinch of amusement seeped into his eyes. I wanted to call it affectionate amusement.

"And with that out of the way," I went on, "maybe it's time we become each other's biggest strength too."

He threaded our fingers together. "How do we do that?"

"Beats me," I laughed quietly. "I don't know. Perhaps if we start by makin' it clear we're in it for the long haul. Because that's how I feel." It was the perfect time to bring up my call with my brother. "I talked to David just an hour ago, and he and his wife invited us to Tennessee for Christmas. Soph, Dylan, and the kids too. And I wanna go. I have no interest in taking shit slow or celebratin' the holidays apart just because we haven't been together very long. So I'm hopin' you'll say yes. And if you don't, it's only because we'll be spending Christmas with your family this year."

I could sense the tension in his posture evaporating, and the worry lines in his forehead faded too. "I'm good with Tennessee. Maybe we can celebrate with my family next year."

It was a plan, one we made together.

"I'll be there." It felt ridiculously good. A plan for over a year from now. That's what I called personal growth. "I'll also be there if you decide to pursue your pops's orchard business. Maybe there's a barn or somethin' I can convert into an office for my future construction business. I'll need a lot of space for that."

It finally got me one of Sebastian's gorgeous, warm grins, and we leaned across the table at the same time and met in an unhurried kiss.

"This lunch turned into a lot more than I expected," he

murmured. "I thought we'd spend the hour talking about possibly getting you a new dog."

I chuckled and nipped at his bottom lip. "That wouldn't happen, regardless. I don't wanna get my hopes up."

He smiled and rested his forehead to mine. "We're getting you that girl, baby. From what I've heard about her, you're a great match."

Damn it, he was getting my hopes up.

CHAPTER
11

I knew my sister was gonna love the guesthouse, but there was no reason for her to get weepy and close herself into the bedroom with Dylan to calm herself down.

Unless she was crying for two.

"Mama's a crybaby," I cooed to Bella.

She giggled and grabbed my nose.

David's eight kids had taught me a thing or two over the years, and I was actually great with babies. I knew how to keep them entertained, I knew when to sway them, when to put a bounce in my step, when to swaddle them, and how to burp them. Get the fuck away from me with shitty diapers, but some spit-up on my shoulder was nothing. Babies usually lit up like the sun right after they'd settled from a meal.

Since I'd managed to clear the room with my house-building skills—Dylan comforting Soph in the bedroom, reminding her that, yeah, this was finally happening to them, and Sebastian and Teddy checking out the loft upstairs—I carried Bella over to the living room area and turned on ESPN.

The others better not be long, though. We had pizza and wings waiting on the kitchen bar that they'd brought with them.

"I think this is gonna be my bed when I sleep over, Bastian," I heard Teddy announce upstairs. "Or this one?" It was followed by a thump and an "Uh-oh! I did it again!" when he bumped his head on the ceiling somewhere.

"Food's gettin' cold, y'all!" I hollered.

"We should hurry, buddy," Sebastian said. "We don't want Uncle Blake to eat all the pizza."

"Oh my gosh, no!" That lit a fire under Teddy's butt.

Soph emerged from the bedroom shortly after, eyes red and puffy, and she said she was just gonna go freshen up in the bathroom.

In the meantime, Dylan glanced after her with concern in his eyes. He scratched his head, visibly confused too.

"Don't worry about it." I walked over to him and handed Bella off. "She's probably just pregnant."

Dylan thought I was joking.

I merely raised my brows pointedly, because I knew a thing or two about the fertility of a Kidd, then aimed for the kitchen.

"She can't be!" Dylan called after me.

"Funny, that's what our brother's wife said the first four pregnancies," I replied, amused. "'We've been careful,' 'I'm on the pill,' 'The doctor actually said it would be difficult for me to conceive again.' Yada-yada." I flipped open one of the pizza boxes before plating two slices. "I hate to break it to you, Dylan, but being with a Kidd means you'll end up with a lot of kids."

Dylan swallowed nervously and glanced at his daughter. "We've been careful."

I grinned and bit into my pizza on the way to one of the couches.

Sebastian and Teddy walked down the stairs at that point, and Sebastian had probably heard it all, judging by the smirk on his face.

Dylan thought it was a good idea to double down. "She's just overwhelmed. Frankly, so am I. If it weren't for you, it would still be a while before we could afford a real home, and it wouldn't be as big as the one we're building in the spring. This is huge for us, Blake."

"I get it," I replied, nodding. "I really do. And I'm happy I get to be a part of everythin'." I pointed my pizza slice toward the bathroom. "She's still pregnant."

"Momma's having another baby?" Teddy gasped.

That brought out the protectiveness in Daddy Dylan, who didn't want me to say things I didn't know for sure. Which made him naïve. I knew what I was talking about.

"Uncle Blake is just kidding, son," Dylan stated. His expression told me to shut my trap.

I shrugged and returned my attention to ESPN.

I wasn't wrong on this one.

Sebastian sat down next to me, and he'd brought the whole pizza box I'd opened, along with two beers and a soda.

"You seem confident," he said for only me to hear. "Are there any mini Blakes out there from your straight days?"

"What?" I chuckled. "The extent of my experience with women isn't even rated PG-13."

In high school when I was dumb and confused, I'd had a single girlfriend, and I'd gotten to first and second base while being frustrated because I kept thinking about guys.

Sebastian was surprised. So he must've thought I'd been with women, even if only to secure my status as straight to my family.

"Uncle Blake, can we watch *Wicked Tuna*?" Teddy asked.

"Absolutely." I loved that show.

When Soph reemerged once more, it was funny to watch Dylan stare at her, as if searching for signs of pregnancy. I was sure he'd get his answer if he only told her to pee on a stick.

Deep down, she had to know.

"This is all so amazing, Blake." Soph ran a hand over the

newly treated top of the kitchen bar. "I forget how talented you are sometimes."

"I had a lot of help," I replied.

She shook her head and was the last to join us—with a... vegetarian pizza?

Yeah, she was pregnant.

"Interestin' choice," I noted. "Isn't meat lovers your favorite?"

She shrugged. "I was in the mood for peppers and spinach."

I hoped she was in the mood for a third kid too.

A couple hours later, it was just Sebastian and me left—and my boys. Oppy had crawled into their new dog bed, one of those designed like a cushy little cave. Unfortunately for him, I had to wake him up soon because it was bath time.

"We're startin' with you, squirt." I swooped Percy off the floor and brought a towel and their shampoo to the kitchen. "Darlin', what are the odds of me convincing you to stay the night and christen my new bed?"

"Not in our favor," Sebastian replied reluctantly. I'd figured as much. He had to get home to his own brood. "I wanted to talk to you about something before I left, though."

"Yeah?"

He better not cancel on Christmas. I'd texted my brother right after lunch to say Sebastian and I would be there.

Percy knew what the deal was whenever I sat him down in a sink. He fucking loved bath time. He could stand under the running water for hours if I'd let him. His brother was a different story. He liked the water but couldn't stand still. He'd kick, splash, and literally try to headbutt the surface.

Sebastian leaned back against the counter and folded his

arms over his chest. He looked on in amusement as I started by giving Percy a good soak.

"Man, look at him," he chuckled. "What a pampered little prince." He reached out and stroked Percy's wet fur. "He's so relaxed. When I gotta clean Mischa and Echo, I end up wetter than them. I don't even bother getting them into the bathroom anymore. I hose them off in the driveway."

I laughed, remembering doing the same with Rosie and most of my previous dogs that were bigger breeds. I'd wash my truck, then my dog in the same spot, just different supplies.

"Anyway." Sebastian withdrew his hand and wiped it on a towel. "I've been doing some thinking since our lunch date earlier, and I've come to the conclusion that I've misjudged you. I haven't been fair to you."

My brow knitted as I glanced at him, wondering what the hell he was talking about. Shit was good between us, wasn't it?

"I'm not gonna blame the stories I've heard over the years," he said. "You know Sophia adores the hell outta you but that she's also been worried. Mostly about you hiding in the closet, never getting attached, never staying in one place for very long." He cleared his throat. "Those little anecdotes were accompanied by childhood memories of what a good big brother you always were—despite terrorizing her the right, brotherly amount." This was the worst buildup. I couldn't smile at his evident effort to lighten the tension when I didn't know what was next. "I remember the look on her face when she told me she got stood up for her—what do you call those weird Southern coming-out proms?"

I mustered a quick grin. "Debutante ball?"

He squinted. "I thought it was something else."

"You're probably thinkin' about cotillion," I said. He snapped his fingers in *that's the one*. "Soph was a deb," I clarified. "Don't ask me to explain the difference, but—yeah."

159

"Can't believe that's a thing, by the way."

Eh, it was dying out. When Soph and I were younger, it'd only been a *thing* because our mother's aunt, who'd raised her, was fancy as shit and socialized in all the right circles. If I wasn't mistaken, it was still mostly an invite-only affair.

"It was Mom's attempt to make Soph less raised-on-a-ranch-outside-Macon and more sittin'-pretty-in-Savannah."

"Either way, you took her," Sebastian went on. "She was stood up by her date or something, and you took her instead."

"Her escort canceled last minute." I nodded slowly. The memories were a bit fuzzy, to be honest. "Don't give me too much credit, though. Dad presented her or whatever, and he handed her over to me. All I had to do was dance with her once, and then I gorged on shrimp cocktail and champagne."

Sebastian offered a half-frustrated expression. "You always gotta downplay what you do. Quit it. And quit interrupting me. What you did, how you swooped in, meant a lot to your sister if she retells the story ten years later when her neighbor sees a photo of a young cowboy and asks about her family."

Okay, I could smile now.

After pouring shampoo into my hand, I started Percy's highly macho spa treatment. He stretched out his neck and his legs and wherever I worked up some suds, making sure Daddy got him everywhere.

Sebastian watched Percy too, though I could tell his mind was far away. "In the fifteen years I've known Soph, maybe she's given me an equal blend of nice stories, worries, and laments. But only the bad anecdotes stuck with me. Or I clung to them, even before I knew I was gonna meet you. Long before." He swallowed and scratched his jaw. "In retrospect, I'm pretty sure it's been about Teddy. Once I grew closer to Soph and Teddy, I've been protective, not only of them, but of my own part in their family. You didn't wanna be in my head when she met Dylan."

I'd heard about that, actually. I just hadn't made the connection between Sebastian, Soph's best friend, and Bastian, the guy Teddy raved about. Mainly because Soph and I had never made it a habit to refer to our friends by name—not since she'd left Georgia. It was usually "My friend and I" or "A buddy of mine."

But I did remember Soph telling me about her protective friend who was skeptical of Dylan. It'd taken Sebastian a long time to warm up to him.

"I think I made you the enemy way back, when Teddy started telling me about his chats with Uncle Blake," he murmured. "Apparently, you were the coolest guy ever. And something switched off in my brain. I stopped listening to him, and you disappeared. You existed on the fringes of our life—on the other side of the country."

An old defense mechanism urged me to get annoyed, but I couldn't. I felt bad for him, 'cause that was no way to live, to feel so threatened by others. At the same time, I knew why. I knew about his scatterbrained folks, who'd never been the parents he and his sister had deserved.

Abandonment issues could sink their claws deep into someone. I'd lived with the fear of abandonment for over twenty-five years.

The fear had been valid.

"Since you came back, I've reevaluated everything." Sebastian glanced at me briefly before dropping his gaze to Percy again. "I watched you at Teddy's birthday breakfast—and the relationship you have. It's...it's very different from my relationship with him."

My question about what he meant by that must've been written on my forehead because he continued.

"I try to be the fun friend who lets him get away with shit Soph and Dylan wouldn't, but I still end up being a bonus uncle with a parental point of view," he clarified. "Regardless of what Teddy and I do together, I always have his future in mind. Every activity has to benefit his tomorrow—like exercise and going to bed on time and the gifts I get for his birthday. I thought, well, books, those are good. He has to study more than most. Skates— same story. Great for exercise and staying active." He smirked slightly and rubbed the back of his neck. "Then you come along and give him RC monster trucks that literally spew out fire, and you go, 'Sometimes you just wanna watch shit blow up.'"

I grinned and shifted Percy under the running water, washing away all the shampoo.

"You let him be a little reckless while still making sure he's safe." Sebastian stopped avoiding eye contact, and the affection in his gaze was reassuring. "He needs that. He deserves it. And Soph, Dylan, and I need to see it. We need the occasional reminder that Teddy's more than his limitations. He's a thriving preteen in the middle of growing up, and you're a tad quicker than us to trust him to handle certain things on his own. That's how he evolves, when he's challenged."

Jesus. How did I respond to that? With those words, I felt more included in their Washington family than I'd ever felt back home.

This is your home now.

"So..." Sebastian inched closer and kissed my shoulder. "It was unfair of me to turn you into the competition when, in reality, you're what's been missing. In more ways than one."

"Damn, darlin'." I had to clear my throat when it suddenly felt thick. "I don't know what to say."

But it fucking sucked that he couldn't sleep here tonight. I wasn't the best with words, and I had to express what I felt somehow.

One thing was for sure, though. Every part of me had left Georgia for this place. I wanted to face my future with Sebastian by my side.

"You don't have to say anything." He handed me the towel as I shut off the water. "I just wanted to get it off my chest."

I gathered a tiny, soppin' wet Percy in the towel and held him to me. "Can we spend the night tomorrow? I'm better at showing than telling."

I would've demanded to go with him tonight if I didn't have to get up early tomorrow. Dylan was stopping by at six to pick up the RV, and I would drive his company car to his office, after which he'd drive me home again. Then I was taking Teddy to his regular school because Soph had a checkup with Bella.

"What're you gonna show me?" Sebastian's mouth twisted up a fraction, a slight movement that somehow turned him even more sinfully attractive. He had a way about him. As soon as it was about sex, he was all power, dominance, and savagery.

"Oh, you know," I responded casually. "Just some worship."

He rumbled a rich, sexy laugh and pulled me closer. "Tomorrow—it's a date." Instead of giving me a kiss, he dipped down and dropped a smooch to Percy's forehead. "Take care of Daddy until I get my hands on him tomorrow, little one." It was finally my turn after that, and he gave me a warm, firm kiss. "We'll talk before then, but make sure to call me after you've met Nala."

Fuck, don't remind me. I was meeting her and her owner tomorrow at two.

"Will do," I replied. "And thank you, you know, for sayin' all that earlier."

He cupped my cheek and kissed me again, and I closed my eyes, savoring the too-brief moment.

Man, it was too easy to fall in love with this hippie beast.

It was too easy to fall for Nala too.

Her owner, Sam, was a nice fella who lived up in Westslope with his wife and two kids, surrounded by forest and mountains. Despite the cold and the pouring rain, we stayed out on the wraparound porch, which seemed a bit odd, but I didn't dig. I wasn't here for an invitation for coffee and to get chummy with a human.

While Sam sat on a bench and chitchatted about the misfortune of discovering his youngest was allergic, I'd gotten comfortable on one knee on the floorboards. Nala soaked up the attention I gave her and seemed full of energy.

She was a beauty. The rich brown color of her fur put her in another category from the dominant breed in her, German shepherd. According to Sam, she was part Lab and Treeing Cur too, which explained her shinier and softer coat, not to mention it made her more slender.

Gorgeous brown eyes, expressive ones that showed she was alert and paying attention. Bless Oppy and Percy, but they weren't working dogs. I'd trained them in discipline as well as I could, and the rest... I mean, they were like children. I could already tell Nala was different—more like Rosie and my previous companions.

I listened as Sam told me she'd been very healthy so far, no problems with her parents either, and she'd only needed to see a vet twice, once for a sprained leg, once when she tore a nail right off.

After the practical things, like her medical history, vaccines, and ID chip, Sam asked about me and my experience with dogs and hunting. And I was all too happy to talk hunting and pups.

I was in the middle of a story of when Rosie tracked the biggest buck I ever brought home when the front door slammed open and a woman stepped out with a screaming toddler in her arms.

I stood up automatically and removed my hat.

Picking up on the woman's mood and some weird tension between her and Sam, I assumed introductions were out of the question. I watched Nala instead, who darted over to the woman and sniffed on the toddler's foot. Tail wagging, huffing, chatting. She wanted to be a part of whatever was going on.

Sam and his wife exchanged some quick words. The wife was ready to go to work, and he had to hurry up because she couldn't do "everything on her own." The kids were hungry; the laundry was piling up.

When she disappeared inside again, Sam turned to me with a tired smirk and told me never to get married.

I chuckled out of habit and put on my hat again.

"Well, I've heard everything I need to hear," he said next. "I'm suggesting a trial run over the weekend while I get the ownership transfer started. In the end, it's really up to Nala, but she seems to like you plenty."

Fuck me if I didn't wanna fist-pump the air. Not yet, though. I was gonna be patient. Probably. I was gonna try, anyway. And in the meantime, plan the best fucking weekend for this girl. Maybe Sebastian and I could bring the bigger dogs up here and find a good hiking trail.

CHAPTER 12

Nala was officially registered as mine two weeks later, and by then, nothing else made sense. I'd had her throughout the waiting period, and she'd become well integrated with both Sebastian's dogs and my boys. I'd met up with Sam more than once too, and we'd taken a few treks in the woods with Nala—in his words, to make the transition easier, but it was probably more for him. It was rough having to give away a family member.

It was also a little rough to realize that Nala preferred Sebastian's house over my place, even though it was self-explanatory. Soph and Dylan's property would have plenty of space for dogs to run around when it was ready, but we weren't there yet. At this point, Nala had a plot of mud and shrubs and bushes with me, and a forest and a beach with Sebastian. Plus Mischa and Echo.

Sebastian shrugged and said I'd simply have to stay at his place more often.

I could live with that.

As November ticked by, I grew more and more hooked on the everyday life we built together. We spent some nights apart but most together, some nights at my place but most at his. If he had to work early, we got up even earlier and walked the dogs together. Then while he showered and got ready, I prepared breakfast and coffee. I started visiting him at the Quad too, so the kids there could get to know me a little. I met with Dominic Cleary, who was all too happy to give me the green light to host a class after the holidays.

Two days before Thanksgiving, I got my first job in Washington too, conveniently with the company that was gonna build Soph and Dylan's house next spring. The builder had been impressed with my vision for their house, leaving no doubt to whether or not I knew what I was talking about, so he had cared less about previous employers' referrals and praise. To be fair, I did have some great referrals, and only an idiot would include the bad ones.

Life was great, I kept thinking to myself. Every day I woke up with Sebastian, I took a deep breath and thought, *it's real.*

I supposed it was only fair that I got knocked down by a blast from the past.

"Who calls at this hour?" Sebastian grumbled sleepily.

I blinked and stared at the screen.

Dad.

"Probably a telemarketer on the East Coast," I muttered and sent him to voice mail. Then I turned off the sound and rolled over and into Sebastian's arms.

It was Thanksgiving. Today wasn't the day I worried about my folks.

Since we planned on spending the day eating until we passed out, we packed a light breakfast and drove straight up into the woods with the dogs. In fact, we headed to the lake we'd visited this summer. With no one around for miles, the dogs could roam free while Sebastian and I found a picnic table and unpacked our sandwiches and thermos.

The air was crisp and misted with each breath, the trees around the narrow lake were a deep forest green or burned red, the sky was snow white, and the silence brought me so much peace.

"This is the life, darlin'." I took a sip of my coffee and peered out over the lake. It was so calm that the water became a mirror.

"Despite the cold?" He smirked and sat down next to me, our backs to the table.

"Despite the cold." I nodded once and chuckled. I'd geared up proper for the winter. A nice, warm vest went over my fall jacket, a beanie had replaced my hat, and I'd bought new boots. I took another sip of my coffee and felt so fucking content I didn't know what to do with myself. "You make the best damn coffee."

"And you know how I feel about your sandwiches." He unwrapped his and took a big bite. His favorite was cold cuts and brie, so they'd become staples at home. He bitched a little sometimes about the cost, but I was good at shutting him down. None of us led expensive lifestyles; we could afford to splurge on some damn meat and cheese.

I let out a sharp whistle when I spotted Nala ducking in between two trees. "Nala, get back here."

She ran back, tail wagging and tongue sticking out.

Echo was exploring the dock. Mischa was keeping an eye on Oppy and Percy, who barely wanted to leave their carrier.

"Stay where I can see you for now, sugar." I patted Nala's head.

She ran down the hill toward Echo on the dock instead.

Sebastian handed me my own sandwich, still enjoying the role of making sure I ate. Completely unnecessary these days, but I kinda loved it. It was one of the best things about being in a relationship, I was learning. To be able to dote on each other. Maybe we even took it farther than normal sometimes because neither of us had experienced it a whole lot in the past.

"What did you put on yours?" Sebastian peered closer.

I held up my sandwich for him to taste. "Eggs, cheese, ham."

Yeah, he definitely wanted to try.

I kissed his puffed-out cheek as he chewed.

My phone buzzed a moment later, and I didn't bother checking this time. I wasn't ready. It'd become drama the second Dad opted to call David—and then Soph—to tell them to tell me to get back to him. It was how I'd found out what Dad wanted in the first place. Soph texted me yesterday, saying she was on my side but that I had to give Dad an answer, either through her or if I called him myself.

He'd never accept a message delivered through Soph.

Mom and Dad wanted to come to David's for Christmas. Apparently, Mom was upset and felt excluded.

David had called last night too. He was opposed. He didn't think it was a good idea if they showed up, and fuck, neither did I, but Christmas wasn't only about me. We still had ten grand-children in the family who adored their grandparents, although I wanted to believe Bella didn't give a flying fuck yet. She'd never met them anyway.

"I'm sitting here wondering if I can trick you into taking a couples selfie with me, but then I look at you, and you look like someone just died."

Trick me into what?

I took a bite of my sandwich and glanced over at Sebastian. "Why would you have to trick me into taking a photo with you?"

As far as I was concerned, it was a travesty we hadn't done one already—that could go on the famous living room wall.

I mean...we'd taken some pictures. They just weren't fit for public consumption.

"We can discuss that later," he replied. "You okay?"

Aw, shit.

Did we have to talk about this now? I'd done so well at avoiding the topic altogether.

I squinted and scratched my jaw. "Remind me again of what lies I can tell and be forgiven for?"

He smiled wryly and nudged me. "Tell me."

Goddammit. I had too much on my plate today, in my opinion. Given that Soph and Dylan were bringing the kids to celebrate Thanksgiving with his family—since we got them for Christmas—I was meeting Sebastian's sister, grandfather, and nephews for the first time today. Marlene, the sister, had tagged Sebastian in photos of her cooking for the past two days on Instagram, and I loved me a good turkey. I loved people who went all in with food, period, and I'd been promised a feast. But I was still experiencing a serious case of ball sweat. I had to impress them, right?

And now this.

"My mother is upset, so Dad's been calling to more or less demand they get invited to David and Melissa's for Christmas."

My stomach was in knots the second the truth was out, and I had to put away my sandwich.

"Oh." Sebastian nodded slowly, digesting, and put down the rest of his sandwich too. He didn't look happy at all. "I mean, I knew we'd have to deal with this at some point..."

I wasn't so sure. My plan had been to avoid my parents for the rest of my life. That was why the whole thing stung so bad, because my leaving Georgia had been goodbye for me. There wasn't a chance in hell I could pretend as if nothing had happened so that Mom and Dad could get their traditional holidays like so many times before. I couldn't. I wasn't stepping into another goddamn closet for as long as I lived.

"It's up to you, then." Sebastian cleared his throat and stared at the ground. "Either I back out and spend the holidays with Marlene and Pops, or I tag along as your friend. Or Soph's friend—whatever." His jaw clenched, and the evident tension stole my attention before his words registered fully.

Back the fuck up.

"Wait, *what*?" I couldn't believe or understand what I was hearing. "Why the fuck would I bring you as a *friend*?"

He frowned at me, as if the answer was obvious. "That's kind of the deal, Blake. I'm assuming David didn't invite them in the first place so that you can be yourself, but if your parents are coming, you gotta go back to pretending."

"But—" *Oh my fuck.* He didn't know. He didn't fucking know. I groaned and scrubbed at my face, feeling like a goddamn moron. Holy shit. How had we gone this far without it coming up?

Truth be told, I hadn't thought about it in a while, and before then, I'd been sort of hoping he'd find out through Soph. Because I hadn't told her she couldn't say anything. And they were best friends. They talked.

Evidently not enough.

"You sweet idiot, I can't believe you'd start a relationship with me thinkin' I was still in the closet." I stood up just to hitch a leg over the bench so I could straddle it and face Sebastian better. "I already told them everythin'. I'm out. They know."

When I'd first gotten back to Washington, I would've refused to bring it up. I didn't want Sebastian's pity—or for my folks to be the subject of anything. I'd just wanted to put it behind me and live in a place where they didn't exist. Perhaps I'd succeeded too well.

Sebastian stared at me blankly, and when he opened his mouth to respond, nothing came out.

I might as well get it all out there so we wouldn't have any misunderstandings about this in the future. So in true Blake Kidd spirit, I word vomited from start to finish. I told him about the suffocating feeling I'd returned to Georgia with, how his talk of honesty and being true to myself had haunted me, and, eventually, how it'd convinced me to believe that there was at least a small chance my mom would love me for who I really was, too.

At that point, Sebastian mirrored my position on the bench and cupped the back of my head, and he rested our foreheads together.

It made it easier to talk, and I wanted it over with as quickly as possible.

My stomach churned painfully as I forced myself through the retelling of how my folks had acted once I'd told them I was gay. Because it'd turned out that the actual coming out was jack-shit in comparison. But then, waiting for their reaction and how Mom had chosen to avoid it all—that was the real gut punch. I was still unable to understand how she could smile casually at breakfast and completely ignore what'd taken me twenty-five years to admit to them.

My amazing childhood memories were stolen, at least the ones involving my mother. Like when she chased me around in the kitchen after I'd snatched a couple cookies before I was allowed. Those laughs transcended time and bounced off the walls of the ranch I'd grown up in. Same when she started teaching me how to cook. I'd been the troublemaker and the hell-raiser, but she'd had a soft spot for our moments in the kitchen. All those memories—ruined. If she'd known my true nature back then, she wouldn't have bothered with me.

Lastly, how Dad delivered the final kick in the teeth. How he'd driven out to where I'd been fixing the fence, the speech he gave me, the buildup to "You do what's best for your family." As in, get the fuck out of there.

"And some hush money to sweeten the deal and to clear him of guilt. Three hundred grand." As I heard myself speak, it hit me how dead I sounded. I'd lost my energy. Goddammit, this was why I didn't wanna rehash the past today. "I reckon you know the rest of it. I drove around for a bit, stayed with my brother for a week, lost Rosie, then came here." I eased away a little, needing some space, and scanned the immediate area to make sure I knew where the dogs were. "I'd already bought the land for Soph and Dylan, and I can't use the money Dad gave me for myself. It don't feel right. But I needed something to do, so..."

"So you decided to stay and build them a home," Sebastian finished quietly.

I nodded. "And because I couldn't let go of you. Even when I was in denial, I..." I shrugged. "I'm sorry. I should've brought it up sooner. Before—when the only thing you and I were good at was fighting and screwing in parking lots—I didn't want you to know. I didn't want you to feel sorry for me."

He sighed and gathered my hands in his, and he pressed his lips to my knuckles. "It's called sympathy, baby."

"I didn't want you to have that either," I insisted. "I didn't want that colorin' your feelings about me."

"It wouldn't and it doesn't." He lowered our hands again and gave me a firm look. "Would I have been less of a dick? Maybe. I sure hope so. But it wouldn't have altered my feelings, Blake."

It didn't matter anymore. It was over and done with.

"I should've asked too," he admitted. "I've been wondering about the money since Soph told me what you were planning, but part of me didn't wanna know. I couldn't risk you becoming a good guy."

Now that everything was out there, I wanted to move on and indulge. I allowed myself some pleasure in knowing he'd fought his feelings for me and failed miserably like I had.

"But you couldn't resist me anyway." I felt my mouth quirk up.

He smirked softly. "Nope. I guess sometimes you win the war by losing a battle."

I leaned forward and kissed him hard, letting the truthfulness of those words settle within me. He was right. We'd both lost that battle, but in doing so, we'd won a hell of a lot more.

"You know," I said, my chest tightening with nerves, "this is an excellent time to confess you're hopelessly in love with me."

He exhaled a laugh and spoke as he took charge of the kiss. "I'm hopelessly in love with you."

"That's fuckin' cheesy, Wilder." I shivered at the sensual feel of his lips, and I was torn by the amused route I'd initially planned to take and the heady path he led us down in the end. Was he just parroting me or did he mean it?

It was so noticeable whenever he commandeered an occasion. Like a flip of a switch, my mind sought out his and submitted to his will. I wanted to melt into him and seek solace.

"Tell me you mean it, please."

"I mean it, baby," he murmured. "I love you."

I exhaled and dove headfirst into the sea of relief and, for once, utter fucking certainty that this was it. "Me too. I love you."

"Good," he whispered and smiled into the kiss. "I'm keeping you on a mental leash today. You're gonna worship my cock when we get home tonight until there's no doubt that you wanna spend the rest of your life with me."

Fuck me.

True to his word, he kept his fingers in my brain all day. He made it less nerve-racking for me to meet his family, but he was a little too good at flashing me sinful smirks that promised filthy things. Focusing on Sebastian so much almost made me miss the fact that his grandfather was a hilarious old man.

I was already a fan of the main house too. It was modest and cozy, farm life met mountain cabin, and its interior hadn't changed much in the past forty or fifty years.

Sebastian's sister was a typical city gal—well, that was my first impression, judging by how she spoke, carried herself, and the nice clothes and makeup she wore. But that changed when I got to see her in the kitchen. She clearly adored taking care of Sebastian and their pops, and she bossed them around much like Soph and Melissa could do with David and me on holidays. There was nothing to be nervous about. I was thrown into their Thanksgiving atmosphere without any changes being made. Nothing more, nothing less. It fit me perfectly.

"Mattis, I swear! Stop riling him up." Marlene shooed her eldest boy away from the kitchen. Mattis ducked out with a mischievous grin I remembered pretty well from when I was nine.

In the meantime, Sebastian swooped up a six-year-old and sat down with him at the table. "Brothers are the worst, aren't they?"

"Yes!" Casper and Marlene exclaimed in unison. Marlene continued as she checked the turkey in the oven, which smelled fucking fantastic. "Sweetie, remind Pop-Pop he was going to tell you another story of what a terror Uncle Sebastian was to me when we were kids."

Mr. Wilder chuckled gruffly and shook his head. He sat closest to the window and was cleaning his pipe, as one did.

"It was the other way around," Sebastian drawled. Then he whispered something to Casper, who let out a loud laugh.

I could probably watch Sebastian and their family dynamic for hours. It was so instantly inviting and casual. And a big bonus—Sebastian Wilder in a black button-down that hugged his body impeccably. It added to the wicked glint in his green eyes.

"Go sit down, Blake," Marlene urged me. "And maybe teach my brother that he *can* actually lose the jeans for one night and go with nice slacks."

I grinned. Funnily enough, I'd mentioned it earlier, but Sebastian had waved it off. He said he wasn't gonna waste his slacks—or dress pants, more accurately—on a dinner that would undoubtedly end with him helping his grandfather with something around the house. In which case, his clothes would get dirty anyway.

"All right. You sure you don't want any help?" I asked.

"Positive."

So I joined Sebastian at the table and sat down next to him.

He and Casper were discussing what they were going to express thanks for before dinner. Casper was very thankful for his new phone. Sebastian was thankful he didn't have to watch football this Thanksgiving.

I side-eyed him.

Since we hadn't watched the game today, he'd promised to tag along on Saturday when we faced Georgia Tech. If he tried to back out, he'd be sorry.

Casper turned his curious eyes to his pop-pop next. "What're you thankful for, Pop-Pop?"

Mr. Wilder tapped his pipe on the table before placing it into a wooden case. "I'm thankful I don't gotta come up with sum'n'a say until dinner. Maybe you can help me."

I completely tuned out Casper's response as I felt Sebastian's hand on my thigh.

"Have mercy," I moaned.

Sebastian chuckled and wrapped the second duvet around us. We were literally cocooned in covers and blankets. The heaters we'd installed worked wonders, but on a windy night like this, we went all out. The awning had been extended too.

"You didn't have to eat that much."

"I couldn't help myself." I pulled up my legs and rested my head on his shoulder.

We'd showered. We'd changed into sweats. The dogs were downstairs inhaling dog-friendly leftovers, of which we had more in the fridge. Marlene had sent us home with an armful, and I kept thinking about it. Despite the pain.

The cold air felt really good to breathe in, though. It eased the ache in my stomach.

"I don't think we can fuck tonight," I said. "If anything else goes in, something is gonna come out."

Sebastian shook with laughter and reached for his laptop on the side table. "I brought this out here for a reason." He'd brought out a cigar and a glass of somethin'-somethin' too. I was guessing dark rum. He'd offered me a glass, but I couldn't even stomach a cup of coffee at this point. Or water. "Pick a movie or a show for us. All I'm gonna do right now is sit here, enjoy myself, and take care of my man."

Damn, I did like the sound of that.

"I'm still sorry about thwarting our evenin' filth plan." I went to National Geographic and picked my latest drug, a reality series about some men and women who lived on a remote island off the coast of Alaska. Even Sebastian had enjoyed the first two episodes.

"There's always tomorrow." He lit his cigar with a few puffs before draping an arm around my shoulders. "To be honest, I'm fucking beat."

I scooted down a bit, preferring his chest.

I easily got lost in the TV show, whereas Sebastian took the opportunity to savor his little drink and smoke hobby, check his phone, and—my favorite—draw his fingers through my hair.

Our first photo as a couple had received seventeen likes, I saw when he scrolled through his Instagram notifications. Marlene had taken the picture.

"We look hot together, darlin'," I yawned. He had his arm around me in the photo, and he was kissing my cheek.

"You have the sexiest, most beautiful damn smile," he murmured. "We should print this picture."

"And put it on your wall downstairs," I added.

He kissed the top of my head. "Definitely."

Goddammit. He was the one who'd gotten me addicted to sleeping with his cock buried in me; he better step up to the plate and not roll away from me in the middle of the night.

"Sebastian..." I reached behind me and grabbed him by the hip to pull him toward me. "Fucker, wake up."

He let out a sleepy sound and slipped an arm around my middle. Marginally better, but there was room for improvement.

I found his cock and gave it a couple slow strokes. It had just a hint of oil left, making it one of two kinds of perfect. With a tiny amount of oil, I got that sweet, intense burn as he forced himself in. The other kind of perfect was an excessive amount of oil or lube that allowed us to go rougher and more carelessly.

"*Sebastian.*"

"Mm—" He came to with a grumble and batted away my hand. "M'sorry, baby. C'mere." He stroked his cock quickly a few times until he was sufficiently hard. Then he closed the distance and pushed inside me again. "There we go. Better?"

"Yeah..." I exhaled and let the sensations overtake me. Eyes closed, his chest pressed to my back, a mild burn flowing through me...and then his hand traveled down my stomach.

"Sleep," he whispered.

Kinda difficult when he wrapped his fingers around my cock.

He didn't do anything, the bastard.

Within seconds, his breathing evened out again.

Within minutes, he was fast asleep and had released my cock too.

I waited for the tiredness to claim me as well...and nothing. I was wide awake. Outside on the balcony, the harsh winds tried to grab on to the blankets we'd left behind on the sofa. Despite the threat of bad weather, the sky was clear and the moon painted the bedroom a pale blue color with dark, shadowy contrasts. Every now and then, the house creaked in places.

"You gotta be kiddin' me," I whispered to myself.

He was growing harder inside me. Whether it was simple biology or he was dreaming about something hot was irrelevant, 'cause either way, it was gonna be impossible not to take advantage. I was horny, dang it.

I couldn't help myself. I shifted against him, causing him to sink deeper into me, and I buried my face in the pillow. *Fuck.* I needed more of that. Much more. I inched away slightly and did it again, and maybe the pleasure clouded my judgment a bit. But really, why couldn't I get away with this? If I did it carefully, slowly...

He couldn't blame me. His cock was made for my ass. He was thick, long, and had a slight upward curve that pushed the head of his cock against my prostate.

Oh fuck.

I swallowed dryly and moved just a little faster as I ignited within.

"You whore."

I froze at the sound of his low, ragged morning voice, and a cold chill shot down my spine. But my cock throbbed with excitement, sending my brain in two different directions. The prospect of him giving me a punishing fuck turned me on beyond belief.

"Did you think I wouldn't notice?" He rolled on top of me and ground deeper into my ass.

I groaned against my pillow. "Just fuck me. I need it."

"Evidently." He pushed my knees apart to make more room for himself. "Can you reach the nightstand? I left a little something there for you."

Anticipation spiked in my blood, and I immediately did as told. He'd already introduced me to a prostate massager and a dildo mount for the shower. He had a thing for sex toys, and I had a thing for letting him use me however the heck he wanted. I got off on not knowing beforehand. I wanted to be left out of the loop entirely.

I dug out a white package without a label on it, and I frowned in confusion and handed it over to Sebastian. It looked to be the size of a shampoo bottle but weighed less.

"Why's there no label?"

"There was on the original packaging, but then you'd see what it was."

He knew me.

I smiled to myself and faced forward again.

"Up on all fours," he said.

I complied as I heard him open a bottle.

Tonight's toy surprise turned out to be a thin silicone sleeve, much like one of those FleshLights or FleshJacks, but without the hard cover. I tensed up and sucked in a breath when he slipped it under me and down my cock, and for a moment, I couldn't stop shuddering. The material was so damn soft, tight, and slick. A groan slipped out when he worked his hand around the sleeve and squeezed my cock the way I loved.

"Jesus, that's a new favorite," I managed to get out.

"Mm, I'm just looking forward to watching you hump the mattress," he chuckled.

Fuck. My ears suddenly felt hotter.

There was something about the sting of mild humiliation that got to me. I morphed into an animal driven purely by urges and instincts.

Sebastian let go of my cock, released a breath near my neck, and settled on top of me, forcing me down against the mattress. His strong arms caged me in. His mouth touched the skin of my shoulder. And just like that, he slowed down the moment for me. I breathed with him. I felt every inch of him stretching my ass. His solid body pressing me down.

"Christ, I love you," I exhaled.

He hummed and brought one hand to my throat, just as a reminder that he owned the air I breathed.

"I love you too, my beautiful man." He kissed my jaw and set an unhurried pace that seduced me instantly. He was every-where and everything.

I moaned.

The sensations from the silicone and his cock stripped me of all filters. When he pushed forward, I sank deeper into the sleeve, and it felt fucking incredible.

"Maybe I can wear this at night too," I suggested shame-lessly. I could just imagine it. Waking up with his cock drilling into my ass, and then the sleeve sucking on my cock...

"There's an idea." He ghosted his fingers along my throat and tightened his hold just a bit. "I shouldn't be surprised. Of course my boy wants to sleep with a come diaper."

I flushed all fucking over at those words. He ruined everything—at the same time as he made it all so much hotter...? I didn't get it. But I didn't have to. It was the beauty of letting him surprise me.

He fucked me persistently, in long, deep strokes, and never faltered or changed the pace. He wasn't in any rush. Hell, neither was I. Sex was no longer a quick chase to get off. I was right there with him, hooked on every second.

"Give me your mouth, baby."

I turned my head and met him in a hungry kiss, and I swallowed his low, rough sounds of pleasure as we made out.

"Tell me who owns you," he whispered.

"You," I gasped. Fuck, he hit that spot—again and again. With every thrust, he made me more and more desperate. I pushed back as much as he allowed and felt my balls tighten. A familiar tingling began making its way down my spine, too, and turned every nerve ending hypersensitive. "I'm getting close."

"Me too." Yet, he didn't pick up the pace. He drove me fucking crazy. His self-discipline was pornographic to me.

Then he locked his fingers firmly around my throat, and I spiraled out of control. My eyes nearly rolled back. A forceful rush of euphoria crashed down on me. I went rigid, I clenched down, I held my breath until my lungs burned.

Somewhere in the distance, Sebastian cursed and slammed into me, and the pain didn't even register. The silicone hugged my cock too tightly, too perfectly. And that last thrust pushed me hard enough up the bed that it drove more pleasure into me. My orgasm robbed me of my senses, and it felt like I was floating.

I didn't know how much time had passed, only that his hand was gone from my throat when I came to. Except, I still felt him there. I felt his fingers. I heard his ragged whispers too. How much he loved me, how much he loved it when I made filthy messes for him, how much he craved my ass.

"Holy fuck," I rasped.

"Understatement," he said, breathing heavily. "Jesus Christ."

Yeah, him too.

I swallowed dryly and waited for my heartbeat to calm down.

"We gotta make porn together, darlin'."

He exhaled a laugh and kissed my neck. "No objection from me. Imagine you riding my cock while we watch ourselves on film."

Oh God.

CHAPTER
13

O kay. Washington was really growing on me, and I'd had too many daydreams of how my life with Sebastian could end up in this evergreen puddle. Returning to the South now—to live—wasn't on my radar, even as a wish. Not even if Sebastian wanted it.

That said, setting foot inside the sports bar Soph had recommended filled my heart with so much love for my roots that the smile was instant. Six booths with individual flat-screens, walls literally covered in college football memorabilia from the South, except for Alabama—no Bama teams whatsoever—the smell of beer, oak, and grease in the air, bigger screens above the bar... I was in heaven.

"I'm in *heaven*." I had to say it out loud too.

Perfect crowd as well. Not too packed—we'd be able to get our own booth—but definitely lively. About half the patrons wore red and black. I spotted a couple Tech fans too, the rest dressed without any team colors.

Soph entered behind me, ushering an excited Teddy in front of her, and it was easy to tell she'd been here before.

"DawgNation in the house!" she hollered.

That earned her several woofs, and Teddy yelled, "Never bark alone!"

I'd never been prouder of him.

I hugged him to me and guided him toward an empty booth. I was starving, excited as shit, and eager to share the morning with my sister and nephew. Sebastian would be an hour late, though he had a good excuse. His grandfather was gifting four trees to Soph and Dylan, and they had to be transplanted right away. Could he have waited to haul them from his pops's apple tree nursery until tomorrow? Oh yeah. But I wasn't gonna give him shit. He'd still be here.

Soph went to get our breakfast baskets and drinks, so I took the opportunity to ask Teddy if he'd enjoyed Thanksgiving with his daddy's family.

"I ate so much turkey!" he exclaimed. "Then I went shopping with Dad and Gramma yesterday, and I got new shoes that were on sale." He continued very frankly, which I found adorable. "Momma told Dad not to be a sucker and that stores raise prices before Black Friday so it feels like everything is cheap at the sale."

I laughed.

"But then Dad called Momma a sucker too." Teddy shrugged.

"Why did he do that? Did she buy something expensive online?" Because I happened to know Soph preferred online shopping.

He shrugged again. "I dunno. It was after they put Isabella to sleep and came out from the bedroom."

I cringed and reckoned I didn't need to know that.

Soph came back shortly after, and I welcomed the distraction and better images in my head. The baskets looked to die for, probably from cholesterol, and it was worth it. A hash brown patty, some toast, bacon, eggs, a pocket with a waffle, and something else.

"What's this?" I held up a puck-sized thing that was—fuck, too hot. I dropped it and wiped my fingers on a napkin.

"That's a slice of heaven," Soph responded. "Picture an Egg McMuffin. Sausage, eggs, cheese—now, remove the muffin and throw the rest into a deep fryer."

"Good *Lord*." I was gonna devour that thing.

Soph smirked knowingly. "Anyway. I'll be right back with the drinks. Breakfast beer for the grown-ups and a—"

I cleared my throat and raised a brow at her. "I believe you mean juice for yourself, sugar."

She watched me but said nothing.

It made me switch gears. I slid out of the booth and told her to sit down. I would get the drinks—and anything else, for that matter.

"Why can't I have a beer?" she demanded. Not sitting down...because that would've been too easy. "It's tradition."

Was she honestly asking me that?

I folded my arms over my chest and stared her down. "Don't make me say it."

That did something. Even as she jutted out her chin stubbornly, her gaze flickered with uncertainty and a silent *oh shit*.

"Momma, are you keeping secrets?" Teddy asked, munching on a strip of bacon.

Soph swallowed hard. "I can't be," she whispered to me in a pleading tone.

I grasped her shoulders and bent down to her level. "Can't you, though?"

I got a glare for that. But she knew I was right. She couldn't deny it any longer; she had to pick up a test on the way home later to confirm what she already knew deep down. Deep, deep down.

It was a done deal. I was gonna treat myself to a breakfast

game trifecta of coffee, beer, and juice. The pregnant lady and the kid would have to settle for juice.

Our hearts were fucking racing when the second quarter finally ended, and the whole bar breathed a collective sigh of relief. Or disappointment for the Tech fans who'd just witnessed their team missing a field goal.

"That was too close." I finished my beer and contemplated a third.

The chips and salsa we'd ordered were soaking up all the alcohol.

"Momma, is it halftime now?" Teddy asked. "Bastian is late!"

I checked my watch. Christ, yeah, he was more than a little late, too.

"I'm sure he'll be here soon, sweetie," Soph reassured Teddy.

I fired off a text to him.

Hey, quit playing hooky and come to the bar. We're crushing the enemy. You don't wanna miss it!

"I can teach Bastian what a touchdown is," Teddy said, bouncing in his seat. His excitement was cute, even though he wasn't so much a fan of football as the energy that came with it. He was here for the cheering and dressing up in team jerseys.

Sebastian's reply popped up before I could pocket my phone again.

Looking for parking.

It was the only occasion he cursed my truck.

"He's parking the truck right now," I announced.

"Yay!" Teddy clapped.

Soph smiled and combed her fingers through his hair, and I

could tell she was simultaneously miles away in her thoughts. I wished she wouldn't worry, though. We were family. She and Dylan wouldn't be alone in this. Besides, they both had promotions coming their way, not to mention a big house. Shit was golden. Another baby would just be a blessing.

"Hey." I reached across the table and grabbed Soph's hand, and I gave it a squeeze.

She smiled slightly. She knew what I was gonna say, what I thought, what I wholeheartedly believed.

"Me too, me too." Teddy flew forward and put both his hands on ours. "Sic 'em, woof, go Dawgs!"

I grinned.

"This is a good thing," I told her.

Her smile turned rueful. "I hope Dylan will think so too."

Of course he would. "He will," I replied firmly. "Once he's done shittin' his pants."

That drew a laugh from her.

"Melissa will bury you in baby clothes the second we get to Nashville," I said. "David told me she's already packed two boxes. And that's just girl clothes for Bella."

Our brother had done well for himself, and had he lived alone, he'd probably have been driving around in a Mercedes or something. As it was, with eight kids and a wife who was a homemaker, money was sometimes tight for them too. But we'd been born resourceful in our family—same with Melissa. Clothes were mended and handed down; toys were always saved. They had a shed in the backyard—that I'd worked on, actually, making sure it was insulated properly—full of clothes and baby stuff.

At forty-three, Melissa was hopefully done with pregnancies. Last few times I'd seen her, she'd been devoted to gardening. My two eldest nephews had helped her build a greenhouse. Those boys had potential.

Soph was about to say something when she gaped at someone behind me. "What the fuck is he wearing?"

"Huh?" I looked over my shoulder, and a spark of attraction and an instant *fuck yeah* flew through me at the sight of Sebastian walking over to us. But he had to ruin it. He was breaking my goddamn heart. How was I gonna move past such a betrayal?

His jacket was open, revealing a red tee underneath.

It read "Roll Tide."

"If you wanna break up with me, darlin', you could've just ghosted me," I said.

"I see you, Bastian!" Teddy smiled widely and held out his fist.

"I see you too, little man." Sebastian bumped their fists together, their new thing, before he sat down next to me and kissed my cheek. "I was told football gear was encouraged."

"Do we look amused?" Soph cocked the bitch brow.

Sebastian laughed. "It wasn't for your amusement I bought it, toots. It was for my own—and as you can see, I'm highly amused."

I shook my head and slid away a couple inches. I couldn't be near him. I couldn't touch him like this. Choosing an Alabama shirt was only marginally better than Georgia Tech.

"I thought we had somethin'," I said grimly.

The fucker decided to throw an arm around my shoulder and plant a loud, wet kiss on my cheek. "You love me anyway."

"Oh-la-la, boyyyfriends!" Teddy catcalled.

I shook with laughter, unable to help it, and hid my face against Sebastian's neck. That boy was too funny sometimes, and he hadn't quite finished processing that his Bastian and Uncle Blake were together.

"You goofball." Sebastian chuckled and flicked a stray nacho chip at Teddy. "Unfortunately, I have to cut my fun short. I was hoping to terrorize you with a wardrobe change. I bought a football shirt with some Florida team too."

Eh, Alabama was worse, even if the Florida team ended up being the Gators.

"I'm so sorry to miss that," Soph drawled.

Sebastian withdrew his arm from around me and gave my thigh a squeeze. "Can I have a word outside?"

Sensing that the lingering humor in his expression was forced, I nodded and slid out of the booth after him.

"We'll be right back," I said.

Wind and rain greeted us outside, so we walked between two buildings for at least a semblance of shelter.

"Is somethin' wrong?" I wondered.

"I don't know," he answered pensively. "When I was finishing up at the guesthouse, you got a visitor." He retrieved the keys to my truck, and I frowned in confusion and accepted them. "You should probably go there."

"I don't understa—"

"It's your dad, Blake."

I reeled back and stared at him.

"It's why I was late. He pulled in just as I'd covered the last tree, and he asked for you." He took a step closer and cupped my cheek. I barely felt it. Hell, I barely heard him. A rushing sound took over. "As soon as I realized who he was, I told him I was on my way to see you."

I swallowed against the sudden dryness in my throat and shook my head. "He's *here*? In person?"

It didn't make any sense. Was someone dying? Was *Dad* dying?

"He's at the guesthouse right now," Sebastian replied. "I let him in and said I'd tell you he's in town."

Jesus. I didn't know what to say. If he was so angry because we'd decided it was best not to have Mom and Dad at Christmas, he would've just kept calling. I'd chickened out a bit, having had zero desire to actually talk to him, so I'd sent an email on Thanksgiving before we went over to Mr. Wilder's place. Dad hadn't responded.

Except, now he was evidently right here in Washington.

My stomach tightened, and I hated the grief threatening to well up inside me. Anger was so much easier, but I hadn't had much luck in that arena where my folks were concerned. I'd mostly been hurt.

"Why the fuck is he here?" I took a step back and placed my hands on my hips to keep from clutching my stomach. *Ouch.* "It's not like him. He doesn't do...that. He calls or..." Well, under normal circumstances, Mom would handle issues between them and us.

"I think there's only one way to find out," Sebastian murmured. "I can let Sophia know. Or if you want me to drive you to the house and drop you off—"

"Yeah, that," I said. I didn't wanna drive. I wasn't sure I could physically make myself take a single step closer to Dad. At the same time, the part of me that still hurt like a son of a bitch wanted him to take it all back. That part wanted to hear what he had to say.

I knew that wasn't going to happen. He was 100% devoted to standing by Mom's side.

"Okay. I'll take you." Sebastian closed the distance between us and kissed my temple. "You've got this. And as soon as you want me to come get you, you just call me."

I nodded numbly and returned the keys to him.

"I'll go let Soph know," he said.

"Okay."

By the time we reached Downtown, the shock had been replaced by an anxious impatience. I drummed my fingers against my thighs and kept counting the streets. Each one brought me closer to a conversation I couldn't predict the nature of. Or the reasoning behind it. It baffled me that he was here. I couldn't grasp it. It was just so unlike him.

On the other hand, we'd never had an issue like this in the family before. All the hell I'd brought home over the years had been child's play—and nothing that'd caused my mother to be unable to speak to me.

Was Dad here as the messenger?

It was kinda unlike him too. He wasn't a mediator. That was Mom.

"Whatever the outcome, baby—" Sebastian squeezed my hand "—you have me. You have us."

I nodded. "I bet he's angry. Comin' here is like pullin' out the heavy artillery. He's no good on the phone or in text, but in person...?" I whistled. "He knows exactly when and how to strike."

I wouldn't say I'd ever feared my father. He had a tall and wiry frame, though what he lacked in bulk, he made up for with an air of authority and an impressive glower that'd definitely made me wanna piss my pants a couple times as a teenager.

I took a deep breath as we reached Marten Lane, and it didn't take long for me to spot a truck at the end of the street that didn't belong here.

Sebastian parked behind it. I scanned the muddy plot of land and wondered what my father had seen. Total mayhem, maybe. We'd taken measurements for the main house, and we'd drilled to get a better sense of the work ahead of us—if we'd need to use explosives to clear rock or something like that. So far, so good. It just looked bad because of the damn weather. And we hadn't cleared the terrain along the eastern side of the lot where it was mostly shrubs and small trees that didn't belong here.

As far as I knew, there were only five trees in total that would be left alone on the property. An oak tree near the exit, then the four trees Sebastian had transplanted today. Two apple trees on the right side of the guesthouse, two plum trees on the left. As they grew, they would provide a nicer view than just the cliffside.

"The trees look good," I managed to say.

Knowing my dad, he'd have questions. He always did. Questions and a critical eye.

On a good day, none of that would've bothered me. I had a critical eye too. My field was full of posers.

"Hey." Sebastian shifted in his seat to face me better, and he cupped the back of my neck. "Come closer, dammit."

He stole a quick smile from me at that, and I unbuckled my seat belt and leaned closer to him.

"Listen to me." His hands framed my face, and he rested our foreheads together. "Whatever he says, don't let him take your progress away from you. Okay? You have a home. You have a family who loves you for who you are."

He didn't have to worry about that part.

"I know." I pressed a kiss to his lips. "I'll be fine. I'll call you when we're done."

I prayed I was telling him the truth. I didn't have the time to explain my grief, and how it was rooted in my childhood, not wanting my memories of my parents to be tainted. Plus, my future. I had parents, yet I didn't...? They wouldn't be there for me because of who I was. That hurt like hell.

I climbed out of the truck and told Sebastian I loved him.

"Love you too. Pizza on the couch later? We can even watch sports."

He was too sweet. He had to be genuinely worried if he

offered to watch sports with me. I chuckled and said I'd hold him to that, then closed the door and began my too-short walk toward the guesthouse.

You have a home. You have a family who loves you for who you are.

I needed to lay a gravel path before it got colder, unless I wanted to bring all the mud into the house with me.

I scraped my boots off on the little concrete stoop before I opened the door, and I wasn't prepared to see him. He was right there across the room, inspecting the shelves I'd built under the stairs.

His hat was on the kitchen bar.

He turned around as I closed the door, and I automatically looked away. Boots off—shit. I hoped Sebastian or Soph grabbed my jacket from the sports bar.

I ran my fingers through my hair and wondered how the hell I could occupy myself. If I did something with my hands, I wouldn't have to look him in the eye. Maybe coffee—

"Blake."

Goddammit. I nodded with a dip of my chin and made my way to the kitchen. "I see you figured out there was somethin' outside of Georgia. Coffee?"

"I won't say no to a cup." He cleared his throat and walked closer. "How did the game go?"

"It was halftime when I left," I replied, replacing the filter in the coffeemaker. He was gonna ask about the score next; I could feel it. And it would lead to a rundown of the first two quarters, after which he'd move on to another easy topic. The house, maybe. The plans. The blueprints. I wasn't sure I could beat around the bush for that long. I swallowed hard and dove right in. "Why are you here, sir? How did you even find the place?"

He didn't answer right away. Instead, he pulled out a stool on the other side of the bar and sat down. "Your sister made sure your mama and I knew what you were doin' for them a while back. With the house and everythin'. She emailed the plans for the lot—it had the address on there."

Figures.

With the coffeemaker running, I had no choice but to turn around and face him.

He was struggling with eye contact too, opting to get an invisible smudge off the crown of his hat. "The ranch hasn't been the same since you left," he admitted gruffly. Then he sighed and shook his head. "*I* haven't been the same since you left, goddammit."

That was a big change from his original statement, making it personal like that.

"I don't think I ever told you this, Blake, but you were always easy to read. You never hid like your sister. Sophia would run up to her room and slam the door. David would shut down and stew in silence. But not you. If you're angry, you break somethin'. If you're happy..." He trailed off and scratched his head. "I haven't seen you happy in quite some time, I've realized."

The knot in my stomach grew tighter and larger, for new reasons. I didn't know why. Something was welling up within me, and I didn't get it.

"I remember seein' you crushed, though." He cleared his throat and put down his hat again. I noticed his fingers were trembling, a sight that made the growing unease crawl up and take hold of my chest. "When I told you to move—" He held a fist to his mouth, seemingly unable to get another word out. "I saw what I did. How I hurt my own boy—"

Alarm shot through me as a sob broke free from him, and he covered his face with his hands.

I fucking froze. Who was this man? He was actually crying. He was coming unglued. My father didn't do that. He was barely a hugger. Emotional outbursts freaked him out more than anything else.

How I hurt my own boy.

My vision became blurry, and the tension inside me threatened to claw its way out.

"I am so ashamed, Blake," he croaked.

Fuck.

Tears spilled over, and I quickly wiped them away. What did I do? My heart freaking broke to see him that way. His words sounded so sincere that I couldn't help but feel hope. Maybe he could accept me after all.

I swallowed hard and made my way to his side of the bar. A hug was out of the question; that didn't feel right to me in this case either, but I wanted to do *something*. I sat down on the other stool and awkwardly put a hand on his arm.

He sniffled and wiped at his face, visibly upset about being upset. "I came here to apologize, not fall apart like a child."

That actually alleviated some of the tension, and I couldn't help but chuckle, even as more tears welled up. For his sake, I'd keep it to myself.

He shuddered a breath and let his hands fall to the bartop. "I'm tired of pushin' away my own children," he said, his voice thick. "I've been so damn angry with myself, but I've taken it out on others."

Part of me knew it was wrong to come to his defense. I just couldn't help it. "I knew you wouldn't have any personal problems with my orientation."

He made a dismissive sound and shrugged off my hand on his arm. "Don't matter. Because of your mama's views, I caused enough damage by sidin' with her." To my surprise, he caught my hand in both of his and held it. "I will love that woman till the day I die, but since you left the ranch, I've had to cut myself in half. Because I can't change her mind, and I can't part with my kids. I just can't, Blake. I have to be two men somehow." He drew an unsteady breath and released my hand again to wipe at the remnants of his tears. "We had an argument on Thanksgivin'. I'd already purchased my plane ticket for today, and I had hopes we could maybe compromise—for your mama's sake. Find some middle ground after I'd apologized. And she... We were talkin' about y'all—about David and Melissa, if they were gonna have more kids, and about Sophia and Dylan and when they were gonna tie the knot. And you came up. She said we needn't worry—you'll find someone to settle down with when you're no longer confused."

I wasn't surprised by that. It was the easy road Mom was taking, to justify her inability to take me seriously. If I was just confused, she could keep pretending it was nothing.

I was more surprised by Dad. I'd never heard him say so many words in a single rant unless he was bitching about politics.

"It was the first time in our forty-five years together I didn't understand a word she was sayin'," he admitted. "I even showed her the picture of you with that man—Sebastian. I told her, look here, this is what our boy looks like when he's happy. He ain't confused, I said. She just turned away."

It was damn near impossible to comprehend what was happening. He'd defended me. More than that, he'd been on *social media*. I didn't know how else he'd seen that photo.

"I don't know what question is more pressing," I said. "How you know your way around Instagram, or how you discovered Sebastian's account."

Dad huffed, and his mouth twitched a little. "Your sister sent a link about a minute after it'd been posted."

Of fucking course.

"I haven't seen you smile like that in years, son." He sobered again. "He, uh, he makes you happy, yeah? It's serious?"

"Very." On both accounts.

"Good. That's good." He nodded slowly. "He posts a lot of pictures of your dogs."

I smiled faintly.

"I was sorry to hear about Rosie, by the way," he added. "This new one, though—Nala? She sounds perfect for you."

He must've seen the post Sebastian had made about her. I'd found it heartwarming. He'd officially welcomed her to our little family with a picture he'd taken during one of our walks, and he'd written a sweet note about her energy, her protectiveness, how smart she was, and how quickly she'd taken to her new daddy.

"Yeah, I'm lookin' forward to goin' huntin' with her next season," I replied. "She's sharp."

Dad glanced at me, hesitating. "I'd like to hear about that from you, not your brother and sister," he said. "Do you think you can forgive me?"

Sweet Jesus, only one answer existed. "Of course, Dad."

I wasn't good at holding grudges, nor did I want any regrets. It stung bad enough to lose my mother. I didn't have to lose my father too, it seemed.

"Thank you." He cleared his throat and averted his stare to his hat once more. "I won't push to include Mama for any holidays, you have my word. You deserve to be surrounded by those who accept you for who you are. But I do hope I can invite y'all to the ranch for other occasions. Maybe when she goes to visit her sisters. I don't know. Truth be told, I haven't dared think that far ahead."

For the first time in my life, I found my father endearing. It was clear that this was new territory for him, and he wasn't a fan of fumbling.

"We'll make it work," I said. "When do you fly home? Maybe we can have dinner together all of us before you leave."

"My flight's on Monday night," he replied. "Dinner would be nice. I should buy something for Teddy, then. Is he too young to receive money? I don't know what your mama sent for his birthday."

I chuckled. "She sent clothes and a video game from both'a y'all."

"Ah. So an early Christmas gift," he decided. "Soph will have to help me. And to the little one—Isabella? What do babies like?"

"To scream until everyone goes deaf," I laughed. "I don't know, to be honest. Teddy's easier to shop for."

Dad tested a little grin, and it was good to see him relax. "It's real nice to see you happy, son."

The feeling was unreal. I smiled and went with the truth. "I'm glad you came out here."

"Me too." He gave my shoulder a squeeze before he spun in his seat to face the rest of the house. "You've done a great job with this place, but I have questions about the staircase."

Oh, here we go.

"What's wrong with it?"

"I didn't say wrong," he insisted. "I'm just wonderin' why you placed it along the wall. If you'd built it so it went straight out—" he started gesturing to the middle of the floor "—you would've had a nice room divider, and you'd have more storage space. The underneath coulda had shelves on both sides or been a closet."

I chewed on my lip and cursed internally, because the bastard had a point. "I was going for a more open space," I said. "In case they want a table or somethin' here." Then I knocked on the bartop. "This one can be moved. I didn't attach it to the floor."

Dad hummed thoughtfully and rubbed his chin.

Easier topics were gonna follow, and now I welcomed them.

It felt like a fresh start, and we had some bridges to repair. Common interests were a great way to get started.

Perhaps we could even watch the rest of the game together.

Either way, I was suddenly certain that my evening with Sebastian would involve a lot less comforting and much more optimistic planning for the future.

EPILOGUE

The house finally got quiet around midnight.

Sebastian and I snuck outside with a couple blankets and bourbon, and we sat down on the porch swing.

It'd been a wild Christmas Day, with kids running around all over the place—dogs, too—music, presents, and more food than I should've eaten.

Despite that, despite how full I was, I couldn't stop thinking about leftover breakfast. It was a thing in my brother's house. For years, they'd hosted a Labor Day picnic and, in the fall, a harvest get-together. Breakfast the day after was always a big affair where Melissa turned the leftovers from the previous day into breakfast sandwiches and side dishes.

"What're you thinking about?" Sebastian draped an arm around my shoulders and kissed my temple.

"Food."

He laughed. "You're outta your mind."

He wasn't wrong.

I smiled and took a sip of my drink. "So what do you think about my family?"

"They're a hoot." He smiled too. "I'm kinda looking forward to going back on the road now, though."

"Lordy, me too." As much as I loved my nieces and nephews, all together, they were a handful and a half.

Besides, this would be my first vacation with Sebastian. We'd left Mischa, Echo, and Tiger Lily with Sebastian's grandfather so that we could take the long way home and see some sights together. Oppy and Percy didn't take up any space, and we didn't think it was smart to be away from Nala so soon, so we'd brought them with us. They'd tag along while we crossed a few places off our new bucket list. Like sunrise at the Grand Canyon, rock climbing in New Mexico, fishing off the coast of southern California, and hiking in Redwood.

The fishing trip had been a Christmas gift to us both from Dad.

I sighed contentedly and took another swig of the bourbon. "I really think we should get an RV."

Sebastian snorted in amusement. "Are you gonna pay for it?"

"Pshh. People take out loans to buy vehicles all the time," I said. "Think about it, darlin'. You finally ask me to move in with you, we have two pretty stable incomes, our livin' expenses are low, and we wanna see the country together. An RV would be perfect. No hotel hassle, we could bring the dogs and Lily wherever."

He grinned. "You think it's time I ask you to move in?"

"When was the last time I slept at the guesthouse?"

"Fair point," he conceded. Humor and affection glinted in his eyes. Other than the porch light, only the moon let us see each other properly. The street was quiet and dark, covered in a glistening blanket of frost. "I guess...maybe I was waiting until I thought you were ready for another conversation."

I raised a brow in question.

"What're your thoughts on marriage?" he asked.

I smiled lazily. "All for it."

I wasn't even remotely nervous or worried. This fall had solidified everything for me. Any uncertainties life brought me now, we'd face together.

Sebastian smirked softly and leaned in for a kiss. "Right answer."

Damn right.

I kissed him back unhurriedly, tasting bourbon and the chocolate dessert we'd had second servings of mere minutes ago on his tongue.

"I love you," he murmured.

"I love you too." I wasn't sure I'd ever be able to express how much. "Did we just get engaged?"

He chuckled. "I don't know. Did we?"

I inched back to rest my head on his arm, and I searched his eyes, still feeling incredibly at ease, not to mention stupidly in love. And yeah. It felt right. I was ready to start a new chapter with him. Or a whole new book, one that would be just ours.

"I think we did." I could picture him in a nice suit. A ring on his finger. Maybe we'd get hitched on the beach where we lived. Maybe we'd elope and then have a barbecue when we got home.

He cupped my jaw and dipped down again, kissing me hungrier, deeper, and harder.

When he broke away, he had his eyes closed, and he traced my bottom lip with the pad of his thumb. "How did I ever see you as the enemy?"

I pulled him to me so his forehead touched mine. "You were clearly an idiot."

He laughed through his nose and kissed me quickly. "Clearly."

It was a horrible time to interrupt us, which was what my brother chose to do right then and there.

He poked his head out, dressed in his pajamas. "Apologies if I'm intrudin', little brother."

"You're not," Sebastian said, being too polite and shit.

"What's up?" I untangled myself from Sebastian and looked over to David.

He came out and closed the door. "I was wondering if I could bring Nala to the clinic tomorrow."

A chill went through me, and the dread followed. "You gotta be fucking kidding me, David."

He blinked. Then he finally got it. "Gosh—no! Not like that, Blake. I'm sorry. Christ. It's nothing bad, I assure you. I think she's pregnant."

Preg...

What?

I blanched.

"Oh shit." That was Sebastian.

I shook my head quickly, needing understanding. Fast. "Uh. That's not..." *possible*. A glance at Sebastian gave me doubts. *Was* it possible? Nala had only been around *our* dogs. Oppy and Percy were out of the question for several reasons.

"Echo was fixed when I got him," he said. "Mischa wasn't. He'd been used for breeding."

Holy fuck.

"He banged our girl?" I blurted out.

"Congratulations?" David asked rather than stated.

"Heh." I didn't know how to react.

"I don't know for certain," David said next. "But generally, if you can detect outward signs, the dog is fairly far along. My guess is you have about a month to go, give or take a few days."

I took a big gulp of my drink.

I'd suspected a while back she'd been in heat, or about to be. But since she hadn't been ours that long, I wasn't sure. There'd been no discharge or anything, just a change in her behavior. Rather than sleeping downstairs, she'd slept next to our bed a few nights, and she'd had less patience for Oppy and Percy climbing all over her.

"I feel like an idiot for not considering this earlier," Sebastian said.

Hell, that made two of us. "Me too. Not much we can do about that now, though." I cracked a grin, 'cause this was becoming funny. "I thought we were safe from unexpected pregnancies, darlin'."

He let out a laugh and scrubbed his hands down his face.

I glanced over at my smirking brother. "Thanks for lookin' out. We'll take that exam."

He nodded. "You got it. We can head in after breakfast."

"It's a plan."

He wished us a good night and returned inside.

Sebastian and I just stared at each other before we chuckled and shook our heads.

"That's an interestin' way to start our life together," I said. "I guess we have to cut our vacation short. Maybe do Grand Canyon and the fishin' trip, then head straight home."

"Yeah... Christ." He pinched his lips together, mirth flowing freely in his eyes. "We have to get Mischa fixed."

"Poor guy. But yeah. Yeah, we do. Damn." I kinda hoped we could keep a pup. Then again, we had five dogs and one cat now. We were turning into the pet version of David and Melissa. "Those pups are gonna be fucking beautiful, though." I mean, honestly. A stunning Husky and Nala's German shepherd and Lab mix. "I can give Sam a call. And you can ask your pops."

Because those dogs would grow up as perfect hunting companions.

"Yeah, I don't think it'll be too difficult to find homes for them," Sebastian agreed. "You know who you should call? Your dad."

He was right. Dad had mentioned wanting a dog since Rosie no longer occupied their porch.

I grinned. Talk about a strange turn of events.

"To new adventures, future hubby." I held up my glass.

He smiled and clinked his glass to mine. "To us, baby."

MORE FROM
CARA

In Camassia Cove, everyone has a story to share
Darius & Gray
Dominic & Adrian

Cara freely admits she's addicted to revisiting the men and women who yammer in her head, and several of her characters cross over in other titles. If you enjoyed this book, you might like the following.

Auctioned
MM | Suspense Romance | Hurt/Comfort | Trauma

At twenty-one, Gray Nolan became a human trafficking statistic. He and seven other young men were taken aboard a luxurious yacht where they would be auctioned off to the highest bidder. Tortured, shattered, and almost defeated, he

watched his new owner step out of the shadows in a swirl of his
own cigarette smoke.

Home
MM | Hurt/Comfort | Family Romance | Autism | Single Dad | Standalone

The day I stepped off the bus in Seattle, I hoped with every fiber
of my being that my Philadelphia past was left behind me. I
couldn't guarantee I'd be off the streets yet—far from it—but at
least I'd see my little girl again. Then I met him. Adrian. A
straitlaced history teacher. According to his brother, Adrian had
a habit of rescuing strays, but I didn't buy the nice-guy act. Well,
at first.

Northbound
MM | Adventure Romance | Age Difference | Standalone

Quinn Sawyer didn't apply for a temporary job at the remote
O'Connor Adventure Retreat in Alaska because he wanted a
change of scenery. He only left sunny Florida to get answers
from Declan O'Connor, the man who dated Quinn's aunt six
years ago, then left abruptly without a word. And somehow,
according to one bitter aunt, it was all Quinn's fault that Declan
had left. Well, Quinn was done being the black sheep in his
family, and he wasn't going to let his old crush on Declan get in
the way of his quest for answers.

Uncomplicated Choices
MM | Comedy Romance | Family | Single Dad | Standalone

When life gave you lemons, you found out who stayed and made lemonade with you. Or something to that effect. And the day Ellis kidnapped me—or rather, he borrowed a yacht and didn't know I was sleeping below deck—he'd definitely been handed too many lemons. We were practically family, so I owed it to him to stay and make sure he was all right. Apparently he was trying to decide whether or not to divorce his wife, so it was truly not the best time for me to develop a crush.

Check out Cara's entire collection at www.caradeewrites.com, and don't forget to sign up for her newsletter so you don't miss any new releases, updates on book signings, free outtakes, giveaways, and much more.

ABOUT
CARA

I'm often awkwardly silent or, if the topic interests me, a chronic rambler. In other words, I can discuss writing forever and ever. Fiction, in particular. The love story—while a huge draw and constantly present—is secondary for me, because there's so much more to writing romance fiction than just making two (or more) people fall in love and have hot sex.

There's a world to build, characters to develop, interests to create, and a topic or two to research thoroughly.

Every book is a challenge for me, an opportunity to learn something new, and a puzzle to piece together. I want my characters to come to life, and the only way I know to do that is to give them substance—passions, history, goals, quirks, and strong opinions—and to let them evolve.

I want my men and women to be relatable. That means allowing room for everyday problems and, for lack of a better word, flaws. My characters will never be perfect.

Wait...this was supposed to be about me, not my writing.

I'm a writey person who loves to write. Always wanderlusting, twitterpating, kinking, cooking, baking, and geeking. There's time for hockey and family, too. But mostly, I just love to write.

~Cara.

Get social with Cara
www.caradeewrites.com
www.camassiacove.com
Facebook: @caradeewrites
Twitter: @caradeewrites
Instagram: @caradeewrites